Funny Love

Sarah Alex

Funny Love

Olympia Publishers
London

www.olympiapublishers.com
OLYMPIA PAPERBACK EDITION

Copyright © Sarah Alex 2024

The right of Sarah Alex to be identified as author of this work has been asserted in accordance with sections 77 and 78 of the Copyright, Designs and Patents Act 1988.

All Rights Reserved

No reproduction, copy or transmission of this publication may be made without written permission.
No paragraph of this publication may be reproduced, copied or transmitted save with the written permission of the publisher, or in accordance with the provisions of the Copyright Act 1956 (as amended).

Any person who commits any unauthorised act in relation to this publication may be liable to criminal prosecution and civil claims for damage.

A CIP catalogue record for this title is available from the British Library.

ISBN: 978-1-80439-761-9

This is a work of fiction.
Names, characters, places and incidents originate from the writer's imagination. Any resemblance to actual persons, living or dead, is purely coincidental, however in this book we have some quotes of famous people.

First Published in 2024

**Olympia Publishers
Tallis House
2 Tallis Street
London
EC4Y 0AB**

Printed in Great Britain

Dedication

I dedicate this book to all who want to find the answer on the question: "What is Love?"

Acknowledgements

Thank you to Alex for encouraging and helping me write this book.

Introduction

Love can be magical and cruel, beautiful and terrible, inspiring and ruinous, divine and mundane. Is it a feeling, motive, meaning, or is it destruction, sadness and despair?

In this book, I will provide the reader with many original quotes, paraphrase and opinions of various famous people who were looking for an answer to this centuries-old question and warn against inconsistencies and the lack of a single concept in its understanding.

So, what is love? Of course, this concept itself is philosophical; therefore I will start my book with philosophy.

Thinkers of antiquity in their works touched upon the theme of love. In ancient Greek, there are the following types of love:

- *Eros* – love with reverence, when the other person seems to be an ideal.
- *Philia* – friendship or affection for an individual who is not a sexual object.
- *Storge* – tender, family.
- *Agape* – unconditional to God, and is expressed in sacrifice.
- *Ludus Lat* – arises on the basis of physical attraction, and lasts as long as it brings pleasure. With the first appearance of boredom passes.
- *Mania* – obsession, which is accompanied by jealousy and wild passion.

- *Pragma* – a phenomenon when a person induces in himself a feeling of affection for a selfish purpose.

«Change is an illusion»
(Parmenides of Elea)

We do not find anything strange in this thesis, talking about love. On the contrary, only a few of us can know the meaning of these words. They know a way how to step over this statement and gain the elusive, which is sometimes called the exceptional moment.

Socrates considered love to be a disease because it changes people's minds. Having become a classic in the understanding of love among most people, he singled out only two of its alarming states:
- *In the body* – it is fleeting and ends when the chosen one no longer attracts;
- *To the soul* – it is long-term and is based not only on physical attraction, but also on deep affection.

It is really simple and accurate. The question is, why think about it? Maybe you need to take it and cut it off, throw these thoughts out of your head, and live? We are not enemies to ourselves, to our health!

According to legend, Socrates had two spouses: Xanthippe and Myrto; – characterised by a complex character. So that talk about love him was with someone.

Below we present his theses, where the first has been changed in favour of a culture of equality.

Paraphrases:
- «If you marry successfully, you will be happy; if not –

you will become a philosopher»
- «Fear of women love more than hates the man. It is a poison, all the more dangerous because it is pleasant»
(Socrates)

Plato, being a follower of the teachings of Socrates, continues to develop the theme of love: «Love is a serious mental disease,» with this statement, he emphasises that love is a mental disorder. Nevertheless, he clearly sees that this feeling is, as it were hidden in different people in different ways: «Love is the joy of the good, the wonder of the wise, and the amazement of the Gods.» Of course, in those days, science and poetry turned to the divine, bowing before God, showing his greatness, and giving words a special meaning. In another thesis, «Love is the pursuit of the whole.» Plato tells us that without love we are not complete.

Have any of the readers visited Greece? It's a historical places, where all kinds of events took place, where every step taken to send us to those far away mind-boggling times. Sometimes, it seems that from this energy you can become younger, and more honest. Who knows, maybe love somehow manages these qualities?

Now, we need the sixteenth century, from it begin scientific tensions, fire and explosion of the mind regarding our topic.

Giordano Bruno (1548), an Italian philosopher, is famous for his theses about love: «One only force, love, links infinite worlds and makes them alive»; «Love is everything, and it affects everything». By the way, he failed to change his scientific knowledge and lost life for this.

Francis Bacon (1561), an English philosopher, looks at love through the eyes of a realist: «The stage is more beholding to love than the life of man. For as to the stage, love is ever matter of comedies and now and then of tragedies; but in life it doth much mischief, sometimes like a Siren, sometimes like a fury.»

René Descartes (1596), a French mathematics, received fame not only in the exact sciences. His published work, «The Passions of the Soul» opens for us a «new coordinate scale» of the master of living feelings. Let us give two of his theses regarding love: «A person has two passions for love and abhorrence. A big disposition to excessiveness has just a love, because it is more ardent and stronger»; «It's the familiar love–hate syndrome of seduction: I don't really care what it is I Say, I care only that you like it»

There are rumors that he has phrases and hotter.

Gottfried Wilhelm von Leibniz (1646), a German mathematician philosopher, considers love as an ordinary function, as a process – the verb to love which, by definition, receives initial data, then it processes internally and at the output returns a calculation for another person: «To love is to be delighted by the happiness of someone or to experience pleasure upon the happiness of another. I define this as true love.»

Ludwig Andreas von Feuerbach (1804), a German anthropologist philosopher, who offered us a question: «Is it man that possesses love, or is it not much rather love that possesses man?»

Bertrand Arthur William Russell (1872), a British philosopher, urges us to live, think and look for our happiness, regardless of difficulties. The outgoing energy is, as it were, aimed at discipline, which requires constant work on oneself, preventing the main human weakness such as laziness – not to be a stone.

Quotes:
- «Love is above all, the gift of oneself»
- «The good life is one inspired by love, and guided by knowledge»
- «Of all forms of caution, caution in love is, perhaps, the most fatal to true happiness»
- «To fear love is to fear live, and those who fear life are already three parts dead»

(B. Russell)

Jean–Paul Charles Aymard Sartre (1905), a French philosopher, turns the concept of love and transfers a discussion into a limited plane for the elected. Not every of us will be able to study his works, at least because of the presence in the description of the words about sadism, masochism, hatred. His known lines: «In love, one and one are one»; «We do not judge the people we love.»

It is difficult to identify the needs of professional interest in the extremes of human nature. Probably, here it should be noted that the philosophy itself from a part requires the use of scientific time more carefully, and versatile.

Simone–Lucie–Ernestine–Marie Bertrand de Beauvoir (1908), a French philosopher. «Authentic love must be founded on reciprocal recognition of two freedoms. For each of them love would be the revelation of the self through the gift of the self, and the enrichment of the universe.»

Her thoughts about love are interpreted quite simple, all this rests on the first rule of the riddle of female psychology – that is, to be free.

Why do you need freedom if you are loved and appreciated

and careful – we would definitely not have been looking for freedom somewhere there, it is not known where, this is unfaithfulness in relation to the loving you!

In the thesis: «If love is strong enough the expectation becomes happiness,» what happiness is waiting for someone?

If love is so strong, then how do loving people separate for an indefinite time? If you wait as much as it asks Dear Simone de Beauvoir, that ordinary love will turn into a legend about two loving hearts!

But in this frank letter, there is an interest and passion, and not love: «If I were proud of anything in my life, it would be of our love. I feel we have to tell to each other as many things as we can, so we are not only lovers, but the closest of friends at the same time.»

From these words, it turns out that the relationship was originally created in blind, without talking about themselves. Passion prevailed over the mind, that is, the lovers did not have the main stage such as – being in love, and therefore there was no love. Yes, maybe being in love and love came later, evidence is the written text.

And now, we have counter questions for our readers: Are people able to romantically seize – to love several people at the same time? And if so, then love will increase or divide? For example; where to get so much time to participate in such conversations, not to mention being culturally relaxed?

What will it be freedom and a sense of joy or unfaithfulness and a sense of jealousy?

If unfaithfulness and a sense of jealousy, then this pain is not love!

Perhaps, there is no more exalted and beautiful description

of love with the other way that the poets present it:

> *If 'tis not love, what is it feel I then?*
> *If 'tis, how strange a thing, sweet powers above!*
> *If love be kind, why does it fatal prove?*
> *If cruel, why so pleasing is the pain?*
> *If 'tis my will to love, why weep, why plain?*
> *If not my will, tears cannot love remove.*
> *O living death! O rapturous pang! – Why, love!*
> *…*
> *I'm frozen by summer, scorched by winter's frost.*

Excerpt from the poem «The Contradictions of Love, Sonnet CII»
(Francesco Petrarca)

> *My love is as a fever, longing still*
> *For that which longer nurseth the disease?*
> *Feeding on that which doth preserve the ill,*
> *The 'uncertain sickly appetite to please,*
> *My reason, the physician to my love,*
> *Angry that his prescriptions are not kept,*
> *Hath left me, and I desperate now approve*
> *Desire is death, which physic did except…*

Excerpt from the book «Shakespeare's Sonnets, 147»
(William Shakespeare)

> *I loved you: love still, might be;*

In my soul, love has not faded away.
But don't let love bother you any more;
I don't want to sadden you with anything.
I loved you silently, hopelessly,

I loved you so sincerely, so tenderly,
How God bless you to be loved by someone else.

Excerpt from the poem «I loved you»
(Alexander Pushkin)

Psychologists about Love

Does love dull our minds, or give us superpowers? Is it possible to look for any logical steps in it? Is it ashamed to lean on love, or should it be carried in your arms? Here it would be interesting to get answers to these familiar questions. Will the accumulated knowledge help to open one of the important mysteries of our world and what will be the result, perhaps, it will lead to emptiness, to the realisation that everything is really so simple that this emptiness will tear us apart and we will not want to live in an empty house. The diversity of cultural values and the feeling of love – this is our singular salvation.

How thoughtfully philosophers talk about love, and how romantically poets write. Also, there are a number of specialists who need to study this phenomenon, of course, those who explore the spiritual aspect of the personality – psychologists and psychiatrists. In this paragraph, you will come across the strong energy of people who have personally dealt with many manifestations of fate.

So let's try to get started.
- «The task of making people happy did not form part of the plan of Creation»
- «Anatomy is destiny»
- «The scale of your personality is determined by the magnitude of the problem, which is able to piss you off»

(Sigismund Schlomo Freud)

Sigmund Freud, an Austrian neurologist, psychoanalyst, is a key figure in several areas of scientific knowledge. The beginning of its successful growth was served extraordinary ability to learning and speaking on eight languages. With such knowledge, it was possible to see the future only in the socially oriented sciences. Like this and logically happened, S. Freud devoted whole life to helping people.

In those days, medical practice was weak, little studied from the beginning of observation, research and to the formulation of theories. "Stimulus and reaction," so one could describe the interaction of the doctor and the patient. Self-hypnosis, immersed idea of a successful healing, positive attitude – were not unimportant elements of therapy.

And in order to find an effective stimulus, weighty arguments for getting out of a person's state of mental anxiety, it was necessary to see the hidden sides of the psyche, correctly interpret and present them in an accessible form. What did S. Freud, by proposing a personality model consisting of three elements: The ID, The EGO, and The Superego? The accumulated experience from psychoanalytic work showed scientist that forbidden desires, repressed into the unconscious, still influence on our behaviour.

All his theory, all research and observation is about love. Isn't sexuality, libido, Oedipus complex related to the topic of this book? Inextricably! And our hero talks about it freely and scientifically, despite the Puritan era in which he lived.

By S. Freud's «The Theory of Psychosexual Development» even a baby is endowed with sexual energy, which is directed to close relatives. The child goes through a series of stages of growing up-from «The Initial Polymorphous Perversity of Infantile Sexuality» to «The Formation of Adult Genital

Sexuality» and with the correct development of the personality, already in adulthood, this energy should be directed to an extraneous object outside the family.

But this is not always the case, these two feelings come into conflict, and a person may face one or more scenarios for further development, for example:

- Falls into a neurosis due to the fact that his libido does not turn away from his parents, and he experiences a fear of incest – in fact, he is developing mental impotence (frigidity).
- Or he is forced to sublimate own libido (sexual energy) into the most ordinary activities: creativity, sports, science, and the like.
- Available other variants, please to see «Defence Mechanisms by S. Freud.»

So the pleasure principle runs into a prohibition represented by culture and morality. It becomes a major hindrance for a person that to live liberated and freely, follow and satisfy oneself of sexual instincts.

«The fact of sexual need in man and animal is expressed in biology by the assumption of a *sexual impulse*. This impulse is made analogous to the impulse of taking nourishment, and to hunger. The sexual expression corresponding to hunger not being found colloquilly, science uses the expression *libido*» Excerpt from the book «Three Contributions to the Theory of Sex», S. Freud.

Of course, if we are alive, then it is reasonable to assume that energy flows in us, including sexual (libido), just as surely we are not always able to be in the conscious world, and therefore our energy accompanies us in the unconscious world. Thus, in theory of Sigmund Freud's it turns out that there is no contradiction that the libido can be in our conscious and unconscious, and it really does not depend on the object of desire, because this energy came into existence long before the projection of the object of desire and also because it can freely reside in our unconscious, where the object of desire has no markers.

From this can be derived some benefit, it is obvious that like any energy, we need to learn how to manage it!

By nature, a person is gifted with a great talent, such as making mistakes, and this actually means that people, including, are not able to fully control own mental functions. Therefore, let's simulate two situations related to our reasoning:

The first situation: If sexual energy is in the «hands» of an illiterate or deprived of social norms of an individual, then it will either be very funny – to the point of colour, or – run from him! And here everything is simple, he is not aware of his actions. The same can take place in the world of simulations, in a dream or the unconscious, where most often all the consequences will be reflected only on this person (there are exceptions, for example: the unpredictability from of the sleepwalker.)

The second situation: Sexual energy is controlled by the mind, and here it is probably correct to introduce the concept of internal motives, since a reasonable person will turn to the norms of behaviour, and will look for some interest in this. Here there is the work of the mind; here there is a personality – which means there is an interest that makes one look for motives. And in this second situation, is loaded a mistake: the motives and work of the mind have a minimal impact on libido – because this energy is our everything, it is integrated into us at all psycho levels, it is present and controls our organs, it dictates the rules for the development of culture, fashion, etiquette, and of course defeats us. Sometimes, it seems to us that we are driving this energy into the bounds of decency, really fearing strength and the horror that it can carry if it is given complete freedom!

Can argue long time with Sigmund Freud's ideas, and categorically disagree with the interpretation of the origin of sexual needs, but you can certainly say that his works turned scientific consciousness upside down and indicated the exact vector of forward movement. He pleaded humanity to be more sensitive to their desires, including sexual ones.

Alfred Adler, an Austrian psychotherapist, begins to talk about feelings from the standpoint of common sense: «Follow your heart, but take your brain with you»; «We only regard those unions as real examples of love and real marriages in which a fixed and unalterable decision has been taken. If men or women contemplate an escape, they do not collect all their powers for the task. In none of the serious and important tasks of life, do we arrange such a getaway» «We cannot love and be limited. »

And here it is a little strange that the author of these lines is trying to concentrate several opposite actions as a working example, turning a discussion about love into decision making. Of course, adults people who love each other, create an alliance not for the sake of five-minute fame, their values are personal and much more interesting than anyone else's. If you strive for an alliance, and think about apostasy with an already prepared list of suspicions or fears, then you just confused the celebration with some kind of failed business meeting. Why worry in this case, such persons have already prepared a marriage contract, guarantees and the like. As for the logic that: «We cannot love and be limited», then restrictions tend to destroy our whole life, as well as protect us from overconsumption.

In the soul, of course, you can dream about relationships, and there our imagination turns thoughts into funny surreal stories or stories from life.

A. Adler notices the following: «The greater the feeling of inferiority that has been experienced the more powerful is the urge to conquest and the more violent the emotional agitation.»

And in order to prevent the discussion of unnecessary negative personality characteristics, he suggests using a sense of empathy in every meeting and conversation. By multiplying values, in the end you can find true love, which encourages the objects of love to strive for the created mental ideal.

Thinking about speaking out opinion of A. Adler; our attention opening interesting facts from the real world of psychology. If in every conversation, we created the conditions for the emergence of empathy, then we would probably now be standing on top of the ruins of love. In the state of being in love, empathy is really meets often. If you fantasise and funny writing, then it will be like this: Dear, I feel so sorry for you, let's cry together – we have love! And now back to the text, true love should not turn into a huge psychological force and transform a person with the help of a mental ideal – so are born radical ideas of a dubious nature. It is difficult to understand, why introduce the concept of «true love» and how does it differ from love? Nothing! True love, due to the peculiarities of human nature, tends to be short-term in time, then emerging then fading away, when the truth does not coincide arguments given – this is normal – this is not love, this is pain in which is present a love – a «bitten apple» that we hold almost in our hands (either in the head or in the heart) ,and what to do with it, because if you do not eat it in time, it will go bad and will not be tasty. How long are you willing to wear these «vitamins» thinking about the truth and lies? Do you really believe that true love will be smooth, beautiful, without negative moments and the like? How to pleasant is it to be fooled?

Therefore, you do not need to carry a huge psychological power in yourself, and yell until your ears ring.

A. Adler wrote that a neurotic who turns away from people is incapable of experiencing a feeling of love.

And yet, some of them are simply more picky or demanding about the emergence of the preconditions of love. They know for sure that somewhere, there is that very true love for the sake of which they have to evade starting a relationship.

Later A. Adler himself, from the position of a psychotherapist, advantageously suggested to us: «The test of one's behaviour pattern is their relationship to society, relationship to work and relationship to sex.»

Erich Seligmann Fromm, a German social psychologist, philosopher, in famous work entitled «The Art of Loving» also asked questions about what love is, what is its essence and what is the spiritual component of this feeling.

- «Love is union with somebody or something, outside oneself, under the condition of retaining the separateness and integrity of one's own self.»
- «Love isn't something natural. Rather it requires discipline, concentration, patience, faith and the overcoming of narcissism. It isn't a feeling, it is a practice.»
- «Love is a decision it is a judgment it is a promise. If love were only a feeling there would be no basis for the promise to love each other forever. A feeling comes and it may go. How can I judge that it will stay forever when my act does not

involve judgment and decision»
- «Envy jealousy ambition any kind of greed is passions; love is an action, the practice of human power, which can be practiced only in freedom and never as a result of compulsion. Love is an activity, not a passive affect; it is a standing in, not a falling for. In the most general way, the active character of love can be described by stating that love is primarily giving, not receiving.»
- «Love is a power which produces love.»
- «Love is the active concern for the life and the growth of that which we love.»
- «Paradoxically, the ability to be alone is the condition for the ability to love.»
- «Immature love says: I love you because I need you; mature love says I need you because I love you.»
- «Love is not primarily a relationship to a specific person; it is an attitude, an orientation of character which determines the relatedness of a person to the world as a whole, not toward one object of love. If a person loves only one other person, and is indifferent to the rest of his fellow men, his love is not love but a symbiotic attachment, or an enlarged egotism. Yet, most people believe that love is constituted by the object, not by the faculty. In fact, they even believe that it is a proof of the intensity of their love when they do not love anybody except the loved person... Because one does not see that love is an activity, a power of the soul, one believes that all that is necessary to find is the right object – and that everything goes by itself afterward. This attitude can be compared to that of a man who wants to paint, but who instead of learning the art, claims that he has just to wait for the right object, and that he will paint beautifully when he finds it.»

- «The polarity of the sexes is disappearing and with it erotic love, which is based on this polarity. Men and women become the same, not equals as opposite poles.»

Well, there is already enough information to understand that E. Fromm, who expands the horizons of the concept of love, is steadily looking for some kind of rational-intelligent in it with a logical transition to the concept of mature love, in which there is no loss of energy, and it is independent and without conflicts, as if he is talking about love as about something alienated, long forgotten and which must be learned!

How can you learn the feeling of love, it is a feeling either there or it is not. It cannot be called in a person on demand, on instructions, and even with the help of a magic wand, therefore we consider such a statement to be extremely unprofessional and this variable interfered, was rejected by E. Fromm in his reflections on love.

Continuing further our substantive discussion, it would be interesting to get acquainted with at least one example of how he sees love, let's say, between two adults with opposite sexes in complete independence! Or from his definition of what love is (a few lines above), one gets the impression that he calls for isolation, and only from such a starting point can one know love. We would not pay attention to this statement if it did not dominate the rest of the text, turning it into essays on loneliness, more precisely, into a ritual of self-sacrifice; it seems, for the sake of measuring one's willpower to love. But and here E. Fromm contradicts own words, either arguing that love is not a feeling, or arguing that love requires patience. Then the question is; what or who must be endured in proposed loneliness – if there are no feelings?

A Promise to Love?

This is the only thing left to do, to realise his dream – eternal love.

E. Fromm ready to build entire factories for the production of love, in order to give it, and get mature love for it, which says: «I need you because I love you.»

In another way, this can be understood as harassment, and where is the independence that he talks about?

In E. Fromm's definition of love, his line of presentation of thoughts about some phrases and words is somehow not completely clear: «Love is union with somebody or something, outside oneself… Integrity of one's own self.»

It feels like E. Fromm is building a high fence in the world of love or creating a copy of his Self in order to eradicate sincerity in a love relationship with the aim of simply consuming love, and preserving his real psyche in case if the partner gets bored the love of a copy of his Self.

So, all his work is more like thinking about how to find you, or rather a sensual false self, in our imperfect world. Unfortunately, in the described model of the world of love, love is too cloying to be sincerely felt and believed that in practice this can be. However, his creative proposed contrast adds to our apprehension, especially after the words that «love is an activity, not a passion.» Well, then it remains to make love! It will turn out cool; let's come up with a term – Artificial (not natural) love. And here he was ahead of us, personally confirming: «Love isn't something natural...»

By the way, there are many examples in life when, from the abundance of expressed feelings about love, relationships are destroyed because there is nothing behind these words.

Interesting to know, can love even exist without eloquent or warm words? If many believe that love is a kind of illness, then this means that it can bring us mental suffering and pain. And this is our joy – the joy of our tears, love can be even in our grief, though it is the cause of this grief.

We, oneself opening the way for love! What do we want receive from it being there? What do we hope for? Can love fix everything, and fill us with life again?

Rollo Reece May, an American psychologist, who at one time tried to gather and unify American society under old-fashioned conservative views on social issues, including relationships and love.

Inspired by Greek ancient culture, religion and scientific works of the last fifty–sixty years (at that time), he begins to talk about many cornerstone aspects of life from the position of envy for successful people (strata of society who managed to realise the American dream): «Every human being must have a point at which he stands against the culture where he says this is me and the damned world can go to hell.»

Seeing them as luxury, money and with it power, R. May argues that love is ready to take the form of dominance of the strong over the weak, that there is a lack of purity in relationships, and that «Love is generally confused with dependence, but in point of fact you can love only in proportion to your capacity for independence.»

After such a fundamentally incorrect formulation, we immediately want to write that love is desire, and the status of dependence is absolutely not important in it – more precisely, love without desire is difficult to imagine, which means love is dependent on one hundred percent and no less. Even if you turn away from love, it has already won and rules over you. Interest is growing and there is no «...proportion to your capacity for independence.»

In his book «Love and Will, 1969» R. May gives and receives love, and also believes that the Eros – type of love deserves our attention.

The book is being written in opposition to the new age that is gaining momentum – where prevails freedom of self-expression, education, and as the apotheosis of all this, to comes the sexual revolution which finally destroys stereotypes, and creativity becomes paramount.

Arguing from official statistics about the increasing cases of neurosis on the basis of dissatisfaction with relationships, R. May tries to smooth out sharp corners with his reasoning: «The amazing thing about love is that it is the best way to get to know ourselves»; «To love means to open ourselves to the negative, as well as, the positive to grief, sorrow and disappointment as well as to joy, fulfillment and an intensity of consciousness we did not know was possible before.»

Further, acting according to the scenario, he presses on the feelings of readers, and calls to show the will to find love. And here self-deception occurs it turns out that all these efforts are in vain because: «Understanding and love require a wisdom that comes only with age,» therefore, such love can come only after many years.

In the psychology of people, is important the moment now, the promise of special love that will come in the distant future is ridiculous and not wise.

And people really need such a long distance to reach the goal?

R. May on the contrary, in this long distance sees a brief moment of love, life and being, reasoning from the height of the clouds for some of us mortals. In his next quote, for some reason, love is not eternal (which is very strange, given the religious activity of the author): «The essence of being human is that in the brief moment we exist on this spinning planet, we can love some persons and some things in spite of the fact that time and death will ultimately claim us all.»

Such a position arouses increased interest among the population, as if perceiving it as something encouraging and at the same time difficult to achieve. The desire to balance everything, to calm, protect and care, turns his activity into fussy work with the same negative result – the growth of neuroses due to dissatisfaction of relations among the population. Moreover, he begins to see as his main enemy the diversity of people's emotions caused by new free relationships and subculture.

Therefore, he has no choice, but to accuse psychological consultants of unreasonably inflating the number provided of individual correctional programmes, requiring them to introduce a single consulting template, as if ignoring non-standard psychological cases and not noticing own mistakes.

As we have seen many times, the authors do not have a single definition of what love is. Each time, they added new theses in their works, wishing not to lose sight of anything concerning this phenomenon. So, in the definitions, R. May has a lot of interesting things for the development of the discussion. For example, he indirectly confirms that love is an emotion; that it is a personal free choice; and that the exercise of love requires the participation of the will.

And yet, R. May is mistaken. Love is not a free choice; it is still a feeling which, as we said earlier, is not subject to one's own, let alone other people's orders or requests.

Of course, we can see the course of his thought in the direction of an expanded relationship to the object of love, where it is necessary to use «willpower.» And this can mean only one thing – love is energy, that for it needs our will to manage it. But is to be the question here: Is it different from sexual energy or is it same? And what is the use of «willpower» (in the literal and figurative sense) if this force may not affect to love at all!

Abraham Harold Maslow (American psychologist) built own pyramid throughout his life. It was a real humanistic game in which, according to the rules of the genre, the main character protects the entire perimetre of his possessions from constant criticism of opponents. Such a tense atmosphere affected the creative work, turning the latter into ridiculous arguments: «Man is a perpetually wanting animal» and «What life is for? It is for you.» Seeing that a summary of thought does not contribute to understanding A. Maslow writes in his defence the following: «The fact is that people are good, give people affection and security, and they will give affection, and be secure in their feelings and their behaviour»; «When people appear to be something other than good and decent it is only because they are reacting to stress, pain or the deprivation of basic human needs such as security, love and self–esteem.»

Therefore, «The human being needs a framework of values, a philosophy of life, a religion or religion–surrogate to live by and understand by in about the same sense that he needs sunlight, calcium or love.»

Initially, his Pyramid had the following topology of human needs. On the lower level were: Physiological; Safety; Love/Belonging; Esteem. At the top level: Self–actualization. From this, we can conclude that in A. Maslow, love is a little relegated to the background, believing that at first we must be fed and warmed and protected.

This explanation is very mediocre, and he is revisiting his work. As a result, love is divided into two types, where: one love is the need to reduce the deficit, which has remained in the same place, and the other love is the desire for the values of life, helping free of charge and creating a wonderful destiny.

And here A. Maslow explains to us from the position of frugal psychology why love should be between heaven and earth: «Love, safety, belongingness and respect from other people are almost panaceas for the situational disturbances, and even for some of the mild character disturbances. » It's definitely practical!

But we would still prefer to see love in the first place of all human undertakings, and worldly affairs. Of course, if we draw our love on paper, it will be somewhere below the foundation, otherwise the building will not last long stay idle. The truth is that love must be behind us, then the security that the author is so worried about would decrease significantly.

There is probably a big difference when something is created or built with love or just without love. It is beneficial, and «Classic economic theory based as it is on an inadequate theory of human motivation, could be revolutionised by accepting the reality of higher human needs, including the impulse to self-actualization and the love for the highest values»; «If you love the truth, you'll trust it – that is, you will expect it to be good, beautiful, perfect, orderly, etc., in the long run, not necessarily in the short run»; «We must understand love; we must be able to teach it, to create it, to predict it or else the world is lost to hostility and to suspicion.»

That's all, the pyramid is built and, as you know, A. Maslow himself did not choose and illustrate in his works, the strongest geometric figure for graphic presentation to all of us.

He probably did not want his work to be associated with examples from history, in which we know for sure that the pyramids were built for high purposes from respect for its keepers, to sacrifice for the whim of the God.

Ordinary people became victims, first of all, those who do not have high incomes; they would never have had the opportunity to love in such a terrible model.

Carl Ransom Rogers, an American psychologist, one of the few who clearly understands that there are only two states in love: either you have love; or you don't have love.

«Love is like infinity: You can't have more or less infinity, and you can't compare two things to see if they're «equally infinite»; «Infinity just is, and that the way I think love is, too. »

So this is just the beginning of a fulfilling life. In his world there is a free education, there is a humanitarian approach, there is no coercion, and there is love. All interest must develop independently without outside influence. He says that we already have some motivational mechanisms for striving for success: «Powerful is our need to be known, really known by ourselves and others, even if only for a moment, » which we can find ourselves.

Carl Rogers is the realist, who knowing that: «It's an awful risky thing to live,» does not seek to teach us love, he is aware of the responsibility for such activities.

Viktor Emil Frankl, an Austrian psychiatrist, «Then I grasped the meaning of the greatest secret that human poetry and human thought, and belief have to impart: The salvation of man is through love and in love.»

These lines contain the despair of a man who was forced to break his destiny. This is the feeling when you know how to act and what to do for those you love, but the life situation does not allow it. You, full of strength, mind, faith, hope, and love and self-giving, become a simple witness of inability to help them and yourself.

There comes an exceptional moment and «Love goes very far beyond the physical person of the beloved. It finds its deepest meaning in its spiritual being, his inner self. Whether or not he is actually present, whether or not he is still alive at all ceases, somehow to be of importance»; «Love is the only way to grasp another human being in the innermost core of his personality. No one can become fully aware of the very essence of another human being unless he loves him. By his love, he is enabled to see the essential traits and features in the beloved person; and even more, he sees that which is potential in him, which is not yet actualised but yet ought to be actualised.»

V. Frankl continuing to reason, he comes to the conclusion that: «Love is the ultimate and the highest goal to which man can aspire,» hence this striving and is the meaning of life.

Yes, it turns out that our highest goal is finding love, but here we do not agree that this goal is ultimate. It would be better if it was the beginning, you don't need to drive yourself into a dead end, and think about the end. Hello, this is a dead end! Hey, this is the end! Leaving this world, I had so much love that I never left it, because I was sorry break up to part with such wealth? It sounds tempting and selfish, which means it's not love. Or I say to love: love, you are my ultimate goal, I have reached you, and therefore the highest goal, and what should I do now? Protect and store? What if it hot? Juggling all my life so as not to get burned, if I go to another world, will I fail my love? I am not worthy and there is no need to be sad, good bye to everyone. But what is my fault if my body is not eternal. You seemed to be about to leave, oh yes, you think that just end up like this...

You probably still think what could be higher than the feeling of love, and apparently squeezed by the «megalomania complex» trying to choose the coolest of the many feelings!

Just do not say that you are ashamed to show yourself without feelings in public. Who knows what awaits us at the end, maybe a theatrical performance or a declaration with intrigue, or maybe grab a lot more, the road is long through the tunnel. Well, it's time to have a conscience and go to the phrase: «Happiness cannot be pursued; it must ensue», it is probably more correct to address this to love itself, in which there may not be happiness, but we like it or so-and-so.

Erik Homburger Erikson, a German–American psychologist, proposed «Stages of Psychosocial Development», in which love refers to the age of twenty-one to thirty-nine. In this range, there is a struggle between «Intimacy and Isolation.

E. Erikson believes that people tend to run away from failures – Intimacy, even from those who have the status of predictable, and actually not yet happened, and he calls such behaviour – Isolation. As peoples say, it is better to fix relationships at least at some level than to spoil or lose it at all.

Therefore, he recommends the following: «Life doesn't make any sense without interdependence. We need each other, and the sooner we learn that the better for us all»; «The more you know yourself the more patience you have for what you see in others.»

On our opinion, in the works E. Erikson there is very little description of love. His is concerned about the social environment and the legal norms of relations in American law. This a beautiful theoretical template for ordering the life schedule, where each stage of development must pass without a single mistake, otherwise his whole proposed model «Stages of Psychosocial Development» collapses instantly.

We don't know how you understand his work, but we really want to build a time machine, and to look did the young Americans of the 1950s, all their youth, sit at home in isolation, about which E. Erikson wrote so diligently, fearing to lose friendship, love, relationships? Maybe them were boring?

Kinds of Love

Many researchers, both in philosophy and psychology, have made repeated attempts to offer various classifications of love experiences and love.

Vladimir Sergeyevich Solovyov, a Russian philosopher, identified three types of feelings:
- Descending – a person in such a relationship gives more than he receives. These are the feelings of parents for children, a adults for the younger and weak.
- Ascending – when a person receives more than he gives. These are the feelings of children for their parents, or animals for their owners.
- Sexual – gives and receives equally. This is the relationship between a man and a woman.

Robert J. Sternberg, an American psychologist, Yale University; Stanford University, his «Triangular theory of love» – allow you to paint a picture of the various forms of love, describing the types of relationships using three components, which are schematically represented as a triangle:
- Intimacy (upper top of the triangle) – a sense of closeness, emotional connection, common interests.
- Passion (left vertex at the base of the triangle) – passion, leading to physical attraction and sexual behaviour.
- Decision–Commitment (right vertex at the base of the triangle) – the decision that love for a particular person exists,

and there is an obligation to maintain this love.

These components in different combinations create seven types of love experiences (feelings):
- Absence of love (all – three of its components).
- Intimacy – the presence of only a component «Intimacy».
- Passion – the presence of only a component «Passion».
- Empty love – the presence of only components «Decision–Commitment».
- Romantic love – the presence of only components «Intimacy» and «Passion».
- Companionate love – the presence of only components «Intimacy» and «Decision–Commitment».
- Fatuous love – the presence of only a component «Passion» and «Decision–Commitment».
- Consummate love – includes three components «Intimacy», «Passion» and «Decision–Commitment».

In these days, his theory is one of the popular concepts that explain the process of forming love relationships between people, and which is very upsets.

R. Sternberg put love into a corner by describing the seven kinds of love. What do you think which love from the proposed list is the most interesting for you? For us, of course – Romantic love, because such love is the most difficult to understanding.

Does anyone know why romantic love in «Triangular theory of love» comes from two components: «Intimacy» and «Passion»? Probably, any of us will say that intimacy and passion absolutely wrong set for creating a romantic relationship.

R. Sternberg misleads people forcing them to take great risks in the hope of finding romantic love, but instead of such love get just passion of relationship or rather, get injured, including psychological ones with a delayed effect of self-torture, reproaching yourself for making the wrong decision.

In romance does not exist passion that's for sure, but there is a desire to create a pleasant, gentle, sensual atmosphere and not spoil it with such a rough feeling, almost a reflex – like passion.

Think about it – you visited romance, and you are nothing to blame, then the situation changes and if appear thoughts and or feeling passion, then immediately the romance turns off and appears the passion.

Passion always spoils the romance, and sort of R. Sternberg did not try to move romance along the left side of the triangle; this is not romantic love, but something else.

There must be feelings in love. Romance is the desire to enjoy higher feelings on the verge of telepathic perception between the object of love, you and the universe as a whole. Thoughts are formed under the influence of morality, etiquette; the presence of the universe as a witness to your romantic feelings, makes you show sincerity towards the object of love; the proof of sincerity is your sacrifice – you give the universe all your sexual energy in exchange for romantic love; at this kind of love always has victim, no matter how much you would like to go beyond communication, you simply do not have the right to break these rules, otherwise you will lose romance. All other additions do not have relations to romance. Some argue that romance is when everything is beautiful, and here passion will again destroy the beauty of an exceptional moment. In other words romantic love this is aesthetics, it is the equaliser of sexual wealth (takes away the sexual even if you look perfect on all one hundred percent) or is a special experience, the development of one's own ability to be a sensual, responsive, intelligent person with whom it is comfortable to spend time talking on accessible topics, and leaving warm, kind memories after such a meeting, what is in the world there are people like you, with whom could be develop excellent relations, of course, in mutual love, otherwise it will be one-sided love to your almost ideal (ideal love does not exist, upon gaining such love, a person will lose his personality, and this is no longer love, but evil; you need to be able to think about meaning.)

The world is big and you are only one, and it is not necessary to be torn apart if there is such a cool feeling as romantic love that does not traumatise the psyche because you did nothing wrong that to receive for this condemnation and reproaches.

This is really a question: you and your partner were preparing for a romantic evening, visited a beauty salon, bought a gift, booked a table in a restaurant and / or something else – and that you want to explain all this with a feeling passion?! – it's dirty and fake!

Or you had a higher motivational goal – the desire to enjoy comfort, have a civilised rest, and create the prerequisites for the emergence of warm feelings or their repetition? – this is romantic love, which is very difficult for many of us to feel because sexual energy is present in our body, it is able to integrate into our thinking, and requires its own goals. Of course, not all people are energetically so charged; there are different moments and exceptions.

The rhythm of life, limited finances never effect on real romantics, who also never exchange this wonderful feeling for a stupid feeling «Passion.» Total disappointment; a very weak theory.

Theodore D. Kemper, an American sociologist, identifies several types of love, based on two factors – power and status, considering that each person plays a own role in life. Let's see some quotes from his book «Power and Status and the Power–Status Theory of Emotions»:

- «Adulation by Fans. In relationship one–one, one actor gives extremely high status to another, and neither has any power. This seems to approximate the swooning and adoration that fans lay on their icons. But it is also the way most love relationships begin, that is, one actor finds another actor worthy of receiving very large amounts of status. The other actor may not even be aware of the first.»
- «Ideal Love. Relationship two–two shows that both actors are conferring extreme amounts of status upon each other, and there is no power in the relationship. This is arguably the most blessed type of love, since each is voluntarily complying in the extreme with the other, and there is no coercion. It is also a model for doctrinally inspired «brotherly (or sisterly) love» or for the vision of the peaceable kingdom, when the «wolf shall dwell with the lamb» (Isaiah 11:6). Whether, this state can ever be attained as a general condition for humanity is problematic. What is not problematic is that it is a transient state for two individuals. All who have experienced this state in a love relationship can testify that the bliss of this early stage does not last. It is no frivolity to assert that if it is often a matter of moments and rarely lasts more than a few weeks.»
- «Romantic Love. In relationship three–three we see the natural evolution of two–two, ideal love. Ideal love devolves

into a relationship in which not only is there extreme mutual status–conferral, but also extreme power for both actors. We know that power enters love relationships, when the actors feel that they cannot live without each other, that the other is not only a source of the greatest pleasure, but also often of the greatest pain. Ironically, power enters love relationships because of how good they feel in the ideal stage. Who would not want such delight to continue ad infinitum! Thus one becomes dependent on the other for the continuation. But, as we know from Emerson's (1962) formulation, dependency on another puts one in the power of the other. Thus the full–blown romantic love relationship entails both extremes of status–conferral and extremes of power. As with the ideal stage, relationships cannot remain forever at this stage. At best, the status–conferral remains high, and the power decreases significantly, although probably not to zero. The adulation, ideal and romantic types of love comprise the «attraction» phase of a long–term relationship. How the relationship develops from there and the problems – for now there are problems – that need to be addressed comprise the «maintenance» phase. Very specifically, fear and anger become more prominent, and sometimes, dominant, emotions (see Kemper and Reid 1997).»

- «Divine, Parental, or Minor Love. In relationship four–four, we find both actors are receiving extreme amounts of status, while one also has extreme power. This is the paradigm for a number of love relationships in which both actors give to the other, but only one is dependent on the other for what is given. Divine love is of such an order, in which, while God loves humanity, God has all the power and the glory (status). On a less exalted plane, parenting, mentoring and therapeutic relationships are of this type. In the best instances of these, the parent, mentor or therapist loves the child, mentee or client and the child, mentee or client loves in return. But the parent, mentor or therapist holds power in the relationship because the other member of the dyad is dependent in an important way. »

- «Unfaithful Love. In relationship five–five, one actor retains extreme status and power while the other actor has only high power. This is one way in which a three–three romantic relationship can devolve. It is a model of infidelity, where the betrayed has (were all known) lost the status formerly given by the betrayer, who still receives high status. We know that the betrayed, despite the loss of status, has high power because the betrayer ordinarily wants to keep the infidelity secret, lest the betrayed use his or her power vengefully. If, in fact, the infidelity becomes known, and the betrayed does not use his or her power, the relationship devolves even further and becomes the next type, infatuation. Infatuation. As shown in relationship six–six, when one actor has all the power and the status and other none, we can speak of infatuation. Against all sense or logic, the actor with no power or status continues to give (or is prepared to give) extreme amounts of status to the other, though there is little hope of recompense. This type of love is common among adolescents and also among adults with a pathological inability to seek satisfaction from someone who is likely to reciprocate. »
- «Parent–Infant Love. Relationship seven–seven, allows us to distinguish between two types of love involving parents. Prior to the kind of parent–child love that is modeled in relationship four–four, there is parent–infant love. The neonate (and for some time after birth) receives extreme amounts of status. Whatever the infant needs for survival, at whatever cost,

is given. But the neonate gives nothing in return. Its cognitive and emotional capacities are too limited to recognise, and to be grateful to the source of its survival. And, while receiving no status, the parent has complete power over the infant and is capable of coercing the infant in any way the parent wishes, although these "coercions," are usually for the infant's benefit. »

Persons who think about love from a position of power and status are unable to subdue the power of love even on the pages of a book, not to mention real life. It's funny, why even try to approach the feeling of love from a position of power, and even prove something and borrow phrases from religion? He wrote about love or about the corrupted and vicious qualities of a person?

Probably such people are looking for the strongest power and in it a certain status – immunity, which is absolutely indifferent to the existence of power with its force or not.

T. Kemper exactly talked *tete-a-tete* with love according to concepts and lost this battle, not realizing that love does not fight with anyone, and does not require anything from anyone. And there are unique people who think that someone can do, and give them love under the pressure of power and status! Have you ever held a manufactured product in your hands under pressure from the authorities, there should also be an instruction for it and a one-year warranty? Keep your pocket wider.

It looks like he is writing his book about services and prices. And then, first of all, his acting skills should be realised professionally, according to Stanislavski's system. It is a pity that this system provides only psychological entry into the role.

By the way, do you know at least one physical love without

sex? Example: Thanks for being you, present now with us, glad to see you and feeling the outgoing energy (love), and please to leave the power at the door. There is no love in this example, because you were reproached that in this audience from you blow power. We do double two. Everything is simple, and clear.

Love has no power, just like and power has no love. Love doesn't need power. People who speak that love of power, in fact unfaithfulness (betrayed) of your feelings, replacing them with a simple feeling of brute force (logically formulated and with the expected result) that can be managed.

Love is a completely different energy; it is able to bypass our logical centre, stop, interrupt even at the most interesting place, and none of the love for power will save your position.

Love is a feeling registered by the body and soul (psycho). The desire to feel love is not explained by the power of someone over someone. And power can be applied to oneself only by logical actions, for example, you need love, please write on a piece of paper an algorithm of actions, how you are going to get love, where, when, with whom and so on. It's better not to continue further, you don't have the power to love, only a vector to desires, and this is not love.

Your desire to get love with the help of power is not even halfway to love, but rather the road to misfortune. Love is a good feeling, and the prerequisites for its appearance arise in any environment (life situation). For example, you've been so long dominated over me, that I like it now and I have love to you.

You were right that did that with me. If you did not manage by me, I would never have known that there is such a wonderful feeling, as love. This said not very plausible, but assumed.

What happened in this example, coercion/experience (for

fun or good), and stubbornness/compliance escalated into the understanding that one is trying as much as possible for the mutual happiness? Is it really earned love, or just an uploaded idea that looks like love? Everything is simple, as we wrote above; love can appear even in such an environment. So far, only one of them liked the strength of the other, although they both have high strength, it's just that the other lived an ordinary life, and did not use it purposefully for achieve love. Yes, one achieve the other using the word «power» and thinking, that need added the more power for speed up the process. But this means that he actually lost power over himself, and his strength was powerless in front of the object of love. How could he lose, what he loved so much and truly appreciated – Power. He just traded the love of power for a simple love? And what did he think, for him unbearably hurts, each time he forcefully will be returning a love to power, and also demanding return to him ordinary love. In general, he will have continual nerves and an unpredictable future regarding such this «not love»

John Alan Lee, a Canadian sociologist, in the book «Colours of Love: An Exploration of the Ways of Loving» identifies six styles of love:

- *Eros* – erotic love – passion.
- *Ludus Lat* – love – a game that easily admits the possibility of unfaithfulness.
- *Storge* – family love, warm and reliable.
- *Mania* – irrational love, obsession. This love is the result of mixing *Eros and Ludus*.
- *Pragma* – love of benefit derived from *Ludus and Storge*.
- *Agape* – altruistic love, synthesis *Eros and Storge*.

It's fun to read about such an abundance of variations of love. In life, people think about what kind of love they have in the last place. Usually, we meet either monogamists who only have one partner, or people who prefer a free relationships or polygamous unions.

Maybe sex is better than love? You know, for some reason, not everyone trusts love, (by experience.) Too long to set up feelings, stir up an interest, and hope that someday it will visit us. For example; above-proposed kinds of love, some of us don't see your own love. They wonder why *Storge* – family love does not contain a part of love *Mania,* if only because families and relationships are different.

Conversation in such cases does not help; partners do not hear each other, and have lost long ago the ability to return the feeling of love. Without the former love, affairs go badly and negative probabilities multiply over time at an astronomical rate. Consider, on WARP-ten you will definitely move in time, faces will be twisted, and movements will be blurry. Everyone likes to ride with the breeze, that's just the stop of love you skip.

Let's see now, in the next paragraph, is it possible to return being in love, and love to original place in a damaged relationship, hopefully a plastic surgeon will not be needed for this.

Limerence, Being in Love, Desire

Buy tights of different colours for yourself and your partner, this will be a flag of love. If you have nothing on the table, then you have nothing to share, just as there is nothing to fight for. Do not hope that the relationship will return to its original place, they are lost and this need acknowledge. Do you know why love disappears? Because of life as well; the fact is that when relationships are destroyed, people see the partner's actions as something that goes beyond his usual behaviour. This new or the occasional repetitive behaviour, breaks your static model, preventing you from making some adjustments in favour of the relationship. Often, one's own egoistic position towards a partner turns out to be the cause of all troubles. People constantly need to consume, if they are not provided with this, then a surprise will happen, for which you seem to have already prepared, stocked up on cool arguments and the like, but this logic does not work, because this surprise contains a mixture of a childish whim in not a childish manifestation. Is a whim and addiction, a dummy, or something important, like developing a theme or motivating for someone or something? Is it worth looking for efficiency or optimizing costs in this? There is a personality here, and man needs something or someone now, otherwise the day was not successful, the mood is lost, but this is already – interest. Are you able to thinking flexibly? This is a game without which love is covered a layer of plaster. Why do you need love in plaster?

Do you love your partner – Yes?

For what! For no particular reason!

What a very simple partner you have. Perhaps, he has lost all his abilities and longer no attracts you. It is unlikely that he will change for the better direction for you. Already tried many times; and all in vain. You need feelings, not double talking conversations. You firmly believe that there is no love, and you will not be convinced until we do not offer to read some intriguing information.

What do you say if we think that most likely your being in love has returned. Is it impossible? This can not be, right? Let's not rush with conclusions, and read the opinions of experts.

In general, everyone knows that being in love arises first, which can eventually develop into love. Experts say that being in love disappears within three years, because this is just a kind of situational trace...

As for love, that here there is also a joke. Is love can be a constant for all life? This is written very seductively for many couples in love, who have not yet realised what love is, and perhaps, have already taken an oath to love forever, well, or until death do us part.

But we went further, and decided to show you a close pattern that the feeling of love often tends to change places with the feeling of being in love.

Dorothy Tennov (Psychologist) in the book «Love and Limerence: The Experience of Being in Love» reveal certain basic components of limerence:

- Intrusive thinking about the object of your passionate desire (the limerent object or «LO»), who is a possible sexual partner.
- Acute longing for reciprocation.

- Dependency of mood on LO's actions or, more accurately, your interpretation of LO's actions with respect to the probability of reciprocation.
- Inability to react limerently to more than one person at a time (exceptions occur only when limerence is at low ebb– early on or in the last fading).
- Some fleeting and transient relief from unrequited limerent passion through vivid imagination of action by LO that means reciprocation.
- Fear of rejection and sometimes incapacitating but always unsettling shyness in LO's presence, especially in the beginning and whenever uncertainty strikes.
- Intensification through adversity (at least, up to a point).
- Acute sensitivity to any act or thought or condition that can be interpreted favourably, and an extraordinary ability to devise or invent «reasonable» explanations for why the neutrality that the disinterested observer might see is in fact a sign of hidden passion in the LO.
- An aching of the «heart» (a region in the centre front of the chest) when uncertainty is strong.
- Buoyancy (a feeling of walking on air) when reciprocation seems evident.
- A general intensity of feeling that leaves other concerns in the background.
- A remarkable ability to emphasise what is truly admirable in LO, and to avoid dwelling on the negative, even to respond with a compassion for the negative and render it, emotionally if not perceptually, into another positive attribute.

«It occasionally occurred, although rarely, that an attraction was described to me who seemed to fit the limerent pattern in all ways except that the informant felt no initial inclination toward physical union. Despite those few exceptions, I am inclined toward the generalization that sexual attraction is an essential component of limerence. This sexual feeling may be combined with shyness, impotence or some form of sexual dysfunction or disinclination, or with some social unsuitability. But LO, in order to become LO, must stand in relation to the limerent as one for whom the limerent is a potential sex partner.

Sexual attraction is not «enough» to be sure. Selection standards for limerence are, according to informants, not identical to those by which «mere» sexual partners are evaluated, and sex is seldom the main focus of limerence. Either the potential for sexual mating is felt to be there, however, or the state described is not limerence.»

See, what power is hidden in the feeling of being in love. It's almost like the feeling of owning property, if we translate our conversation into the plane of consumption, and real life. The only thing that does not fully fit with our example is the last paragraph, which says that negative events tend to be interpreted (by a person of being in love) in favour of a positive one.

Much becomes obvious, even when the partners claim that they have not experienced a feeling of love for a long time, this does not mean that all their feelings have gone out, otherwise what is the point in the initiated everyday conversations about the lack of love?

Perhaps, they want to speak not about love, but about some necessary desires, for which they have to fight for in the negotiation process, and not make concessions to the competing side? No or most likely yes?

A person who does not accept arguments and position from a person who loves him? Who is such a person?

Love and being in love are far from comfortable feelings. On the contrary, it is only in opposites that people notice the new, special and original. Agree it will be very strange to see young people in perfect order, without emotional swings. The older generation, of course, wants increased comfort in relationships, but then it turns out that they are trying to meet old age, and logically complete their life cycle. So correct, that we don't even have the right to write about this.

Being in love is good, we do not lose it, it makes a lazy body get up and feel love.

D. Tennov informs us that being in love without sexual behaviour is a fake, therefore sexual pleasure must prevail in partnerships, otherwise you yourself refuse love, and being in love and demand them from a partner who, in your egoistic argument, should have done something many years ago, for to keep the feeling of love. Please don't justify yourself infinitely correct social behaviour to the detriment of a feeling of love. This does not mean that you can offence against the rules of decency in front of people, no. We say that there are many ways to create an attractive personality psych type – because, as we wrote earlier: love cannot be created, it can only come.

By the way, you paid attention to the remark that being in love must be accompanied by sexual interest, otherwise it turns out to be a fake being in love. For example, for some of us it exists just being in love, without falsehood. We may well be in love with a real person throughout our lives, never having a sexual experience with him. Yes, we like...both the aesthetics and energy emanating from the object of being in love, and in our thoughts, there may periodically surface desires to unite, how to be imbued, and get the «best» memory that we will cherish. Nevertheless, in the first approximation, it seems to us that such a one-sided desire of a person to keep being in love is not a fully-fledged model, but for the owner of this feeling it is absolutely real and sufficient.

Years go by pass, being in love does not develop into love, but remains the same first-class being in love, sometimes even losing the sexual close aspect of this meaning, as if having the beginning of the birth of feelings, not sexual being in love, or having the beginning of the birth of feelings sexual being in love, which later transforms into other important feelings for the subject, and possibly supplementing them, for example, with aesthetics and eroticism, or without the last condition.

Imagine a person from our example has been being in love all his life, and can easily fall in love with others. It just blows mind from the palette of emotional experiences. People can really experience several being in love in parallel, and it would be strange to call it an unfaithfulness of all feelings and loved ones, because feelings are not subordinate to us. Yes, in youth, people fall in love with sexual interest, and it is obvious that being in love can go into the stage of non-sexual being in love – which seems to be a close experience to romantic love. The advantages of such love…and that no one will take it away from you and spoil it (here it is appropriate to recall the one-sided love for your almost ideal). Non-sexual being in love lives and develops in parallel with you, and this is not a deviation from the norm, this is close to the conscience which wants to have access to the pleasure centre, in order to peep what happens there when it is not there. And it's not sex. Yes, secrets known only to you should always be. Why devastate your inner world, or play on emotions, using truth or lies in relation to a partner.

Now, you probably want to see; what is the difference between feeling non-sexual being in love and romantic love?

For us, not sexual being in love is being in love. We are not looking for borders or moments of times, when and how long lasts the impulse of sexual energy or other interest. This feeling that came to you by itself with its own set for the entertainment of your psychophysical properties.

Romantic love is as like being in love – this is a gift of nature for people. Exactly, a people modified it beyond recognition, and now pass it off as the original. In the pursuit of such fiction, many of us do not notice that we receive feelings that cannot be cherished throughout life. But, yes, if you to sense romantic love, that from this feeling is almost impossible to leave. It will accompany you all your life.

In being in love, a person does not have the right to choose to fall in love or not fall in love (as saying, you can't ordered of the feelings).

Not sexual being in love is when dominated feelings of respect, deep understanding, like-minded views, experience, and the like, but not in order to be closer to scientific, rather, such being in love is a aspiration from loneliness to the desire to be useful to someone in life, in demand as an interlocutor who wants to leave warm and kind memories after oneself departure.

Romantic being in love is a feeling about something great, beautiful, in common, where is something that asks to maintain and continue relationships without sexual dialogue. Here you know that something happened in your relationship, and it cement the feelings in a special way. From the side, witnesses see drama, but it is not. You are happy, romance is driving you.

And then even more difficult. You can be being in love to a person with your sexual interest and trialing to him a romantic feelings that do not involve sex, it means you have two parallel being in love. Most likely in such a situation you will violate the rule of sacrifice, in favour of intimacy, because modern romance this is – sex. Those who in such a situation overpower sexual energy in favour of romantic relationships can create the preconditions for the emergence of romantic love – being in love for many years. This will become a parallel life line, a beautiful story of warm feelings, which not will seek to interfere with you personally in new or older relationships, love.

In romantic love, it is impossible to create a full-fledged family. It has a different line of feelings. Perhaps, with age when your children grow up, you will feel something similar, a romantic unity with a person who loves you, the stars and the universe will be near again, but this is not romantic love. Here is there's no sacrifice, you together haven't given up something important to the universe…to the senses. Therefore, rejoice in what you already have, and maybe you didn't need romantic love, which will forever remain in the hands of simple romantics.

Consider a family situation where one partner has (on the side) an open non-sexual romantic being in love for a person from an earlier or present time, and the second partner has a deficit of some romantic feelings. This produces a devastating effect. A «romantic person» does not experience a deficiency of feelings, but pass them to his «family partner» cannot for many reasons, close and known only to him. The second partner begins to talk and hint about the lack of emotions and the inability to communicate in any other way than banal sex. Here, we are talking about the fact that the romantic partner actually interacts with two completely different personalities, of course, if their relationship is active to the present. It is necessary to understand that the romance partner has one personality, certainly a real one – a family partner, but the second person with whom he has a romantic being in love can be a one-sided, almost idealised information trace from previously interrupted relationships.)

Therefore, for the second family partner, such relationships, built only on the model of sex – are burdensome. If in family relationships both partners have a romantic being in love (on the side), then they should not experience a deficit of warm feelings in their family love. Remember, that romantic love, more precisely for us romantic being in love, appears only between people who exclude sex in their relationship.

Romantics have even more interesting stunning cases, for example, when they expect from their future romantic being in love with a new – fictional partner who is already beginning to exist close to them!

Imagination is vital for the development of thinking, feelings, and of course the regulation of mood.

Sorry, it would be more correct to write all this at the beginning of the book, supplementing it with a warning addressed to unprepared married couples. That's funny love, what can you do. Romantics are self-sufficient, in fact, just a little that can prevent them to living in their own interesting world, and flying high in the clouds. Nevertheless, they may well cement their relationship by creating a family of two people, where, as we have already said, other feelings prevail than in family love.

People definitely have the gift of magnetism, they simply cannot live differently, while some are limited to balanced and reasoned actions that exclude sexual contacts, others, on the contrary, live in free relationships and listen to complaints and reproaches from their opponents about the insufficient level of intellectual development, communication and culture in general. Most often, both partners begin a full-fledged relationship, and then one of them leaves the sexual life. Truth, lies, hypocrisy! What is there to grieve about related feelings? Some like adult television, while others like news on the radio. These are extremes, there is no average.

The partner should have a full life, and not a squeezed walk to the level of Mother's care – this is a completely another love.

The next, we propose to get acquainted with sexuality. To do this, you will have to pass a small but boring linguistic test. If you are able to produce the sound – [O:], then there is nothing to worry about this.

Do you know how many words people use in everyday life? No more than three hundred, and even then almost all of them refer to a biting pet with a tail, and the rest of the words for communication between people have now been replaced by «Emoji» The sexy voice is very different from the usual, try to say or read something sexual! No, please stop. If the walls have ears, then your career will be suffered. Such texts are available to a chosen one's few.

Psychologists from the United States analyse the voices of being in love couples and found a correlation in the tone of the voice. The subjects adjusted their voice, making it similar to the voice of a partner. It is clear that here we are talking about the desire to please (like) each other, and it is unlikely that at this stage in the development of relations they will use sexual bright simulated communication. And it's really creepy. For example, we would like to know if you have experienced an orgasm from sexual phrases and words. This behaviour is very common. Funny, sweat, let's continue.

Communication was originally invented by people for survival, and therefore it is considered by us as an important element of logic and efficiency to achieve the goal in everyday affairs.

In sexuality, communication is a game. The more intricate the person, the more difficult it is to switch to a fun topic. Sigismund Freud wrote that people from high society choose people from lower society for sexual behaviour, because they are not able to overpower their own psycho to communicate on frank topics while remaining surrounded by high society. It turns out that two adult intellectually developed people are not capable of sexual conversation? Interestingly, their vocabulary consists of diminutive words: bunny, kitten, elephant calf, fluffy, sweet, or of official form: by name and surname? And then what to say in continuation: do you remember how at the last time or let's repeat the moment? Super, it is intellectuel; such spoken words are very funny. You understand that sexuality is a quality that you can come to yourself or copy from someone. How many people are there who will choose the topic about washing powder while driving to the store? If you are getting on like this, it is a black streak of your life. Try to go to another place, if the conversation will be again about washing powder then you have a big wash, and then there will be drying and smoothing.

Visuality in sexuality is the next important factor. Appearance, posture, movements, look – produce a fantastic effect on people. Do you walk just like that or do you have several gaits for different occasions of life? One universal gait is the level of an all-terrain vehicle; it is desirable to master something else.

Michael R. Liebowitz in the book «The Chemistry of Love» claims that if we notice an attractive person, then visual stimuli to activate the synthesis of endorphins, which create in the brain centre a feeling of euphoria, pleasure, that is increase dependence.

The effect is really strong; the partners are not able to hide the fact that they saw a beautiful person somewhere. The striving for beauty, on the contrary, provokes them to share information using verbal and non-verbal communication. If you can carry on a dialogue, see what is happening around you then need to ask, can you show yourself?

For sexuality, there are requirements from which you can't hide in a cafe, chewing on owned stress. This is definitely a call to reconsider common values in support of natural beauty. Sport is an effective intermediary for dialogue on the language of body. Not any talk will not help if the partner himself or with the help of others has raised the level of beauty. The gym and outdoor workouts revitalise people, for some reason, partners are offended to the truth being told. This is love, this is care. What is wrong to propose for you? Something that is not achievable because you are weak in this matter or because you think that if there is love, then it is necessary to accept a person as he is? Why do you need a person who accepts, understands and agrees in everything! If you yourself know everything and know how, then any partner will be always interfering in your affairs.

Zick Rubin, an American psychologist, with a little psychological research a received data from which it can be concluded that couples in love when talking, look at each other twice time a long then ordinary people.

And what are they looking at for so long? Face, eyes, hands and shoes. This is a scheme for defining an object – that is, we must immediately understand where a person has a beginning and where an end. Well, it's hard for us to say how you like to look at people and scan them from top to bottom or from bottom to top. Maybe, fashionable shoes on a person scream loudly – look at me from the bottom up, and while you look up, thinking how cool I am in general! And then you put your shoes for show as if demanding to check out the beautiful! A little more, and you can do fetishism. Someone else, the first case see in a person is the middle of the body – the tummy and the navel hidden under the clothes. This sensual centre of touch of the world has a huge supply and potential for love to eat slowly. Partners begin to compete in gastronomic areas, and love is beautiful.

Sex is a small bonus at the end of the working day, or when the biological clock coincides. It's terrible if there is no direct, short dialogue and an easy non-trauma-dangerous mutual decision. Demanding a dangerous game is not correct, believe us, you will not be able to justify your risky behaviour. What seems interesting now in just a few moments will lead to loss of positive energy, confidence in the correctness of oneself action. Stress and obsessive thoughts about the caused inconvenience are not the way of a real relationship. Cruelty should never be. Such feeling cannot be controlled; it cannot be imitated and is not a stimulating tool for achieving psychophysical relaxation.

Dating

If you have learned to communicate, see and show then everything is very simple, you will understand that acquaint better is by recommendation. It is not allowed to do this at bus stops and on the Internet too. This is a means from the hopelessness of your situation? Really is it so bad? Where do you live? You think people on the Internet are completely different? Cool! My name is Laura, I'm thirty one years old, and I want to meet a middle-aged man without bad habits, for a serious relationship...

The Matrix will envy the accuracy of technogenic thought. My name is Sam, I am thirty five years old, wealthy (apartment, country house, prestigious job). I am looking for a middle-aged lady for to creating a family...

That closer the feelings between people, then more expensive will be parting, and the sun a little later will swallow the planet Earth, and therefore you can even get to know each other on the ladder of a spaceship.

Let's make an artistic digression.

The Night Sky

Hello! Do you know that astronomers are determine the Earth is an iron, and among you? The level of progress has reached the point where some people want to leave the Earth and to fly on Mars. Are they bored here? Imagine how many interesting things you can find there: stones, sand and even ice if you really to try. What if on Mars live a Bigfoot, which has never seen an earthling before? How much joy wills to have each of them, need to take an electric guitar, the music sounds rich, reflecting from such a fuss. And more you can also pack a thong in a travel case and buy tickets on a sea Martian cruise. Romance! The stars seem closer, stretch your hands up and touch them all like in a clothing store when the choice falls on your cozy sweater, in which it is comfortable to dream about those places that you have never visited before. There are stored our life, adventures, girls and brave guys, who ready to come for the rescue. And help is always needed. Is there a place on Mars for such exotics? Robots are protect people, everything is calculated and under control. Until the air generators pump up the atmosphere, are allowed to laugh only after the factory horn, at once.

Our theme is romance, and where there is romance, there should always be factories and railway stations. Well, at least one station. Hours and timetables and lighting, so passengers (how do you say) it don't feeling a homesickness. It's sad, because trains don't go there. Promised to come up something, but ended up painted the bench on the platform. Imagine, a friend told me such a story, he was there, he was very pleased, and the service is five stars! Precisely, them there are more, just too lazy to mark all the stars on the smartphone screen. He says there is a new scale of pleasure – happy as an elephant. So what is this nostalgia for the Earth? No, this is nostalgia for Mars!

Okay, I believe. And, what else interesting do you have? Climbing a mountain-volcano Olympus Mons! This is our favourite activity. The mountain is tall, at ascent – calories burn. By the way, there are several routes. The most fun is the route of laughter. People dress up in funny costumes and try to climb to the top of the mountain, incidentally which is more than twenty-one kilometres. The winners are receiving terrible lines of laughter on their faces, it's a grueling sport, there's nothing funny about it. Do not laugh! Oh, you definitely haven't heard the story about round glasses. So one tourist put on round sunglasses and succeeded to overcome the peak. He was not lucky, to the wrinkles of laughter added…mm, you know, when a tan is very noticeable. Why isn't this funny? After all, no one was hurt!

So, you are aware that in the night sky everything becomes clear, begin to understand that on Earth it is more interesting than here.

Aliens among People

Mum, I'm telling you: I'm going to Earth with my friends. It's cool there. Just for a few days. We will live at the Saturn sons in a flying saucer.

We are not vagabonds; we are aliens, as the earthlings call us. They are funny; each of them has an annual subscription to a dream. Without this subscription, you can't lie down and sleep on the bed.

So! What's next? Well, you were talking about earthlings, remember? Yes, I remember, I told about how delicious they are, especially when they sleep. Just kidding, we didn't eat them, really! Trust me!

Many years ago I was left on many early planets in many galaxies for the purpose of some scientific knowledge which I am unable to recall. One of the planets of my stay was the planet Earth. I have always considered myself an alien, although the people of around me only smiled at this statement. And now, I hang out here among people realizing that I can't build a spaceship class of galaxy, because on Earth there is no special crystal-lens that burns through space matter, and allows the ship to moving without significant overloads. Yes, I looking no different from a human, and that's good. There are no feeling because I am disassembled, thoughts are spinning in my mind about what I cannot achieve, although I know what I want and how to do it.

This is like, I'm stumbling on a shallow world, and I'm

artificially abandoned here, I can't accept all this, I'm damn upset, but I won't utter my emotions even once, and I won't burn with fire inside. Time is passes and I don't have enough time to reach my dreams, so that with the help of it I can find myself.

So, we glad to go over for dating, or rather beauty, sexuality, mysticism and inexplicable energy.
Quote:
- «*We choose not randomly each other. We meet only those who already exists in our subconscious*»
(S. Freud)

Intellectually developed people know how to get meet and maintain a conversation at a comfortable level, but this is not enough to create a special interest to such a person. Do you really think dinosaurs are extinct? Maybe they evolved into birds and humans? Now on the planet is dominate humans, but before dominated dinosaurs! There is definitely something in this.

What is the purpose of finding a partner? Many claim – in order to avoid loneliness, but this is not that. In fact, people want to have a similar person near to themselves so that together feeling the pressure of life on self-shoulders. This is a real desire to watch how one of the partners is flattened, and when by the standards of the other partner, the pressure reaches its maximum, then only then can arise (wake up) a certain conscience, which will be forcing a person to provide assistance in exchange for a service. If this moment is missed, then ensue occur the opposite reaction, the partner will unilaterally leave the relationship, because his does not need a pancake.

Whispers. It's just that people don't do anything, and if they do then other people cannot be explained that your activity is without means or gratuitous. Let's say, you fell in love with someone, you experience those psychophysical states which we described above in the book. For you, of course, is not enough that are your condition is well or badly! Your irritated mind will seek to provoke the other person in this nonsense. You are driven by a simple excuse – and what's wrong with that if I do it only in good intentions! Do you care? Are you an egoist? You think about your needs and make cunning plans to get the interested object of love. The phrase «for the sake of love» always sounds rough for love, and now it is obvious on the one hundred per cent. Therefore, we ask ourselves the question: How to meet a person, keeping «compensation» (individual should not feel discomfort from your pressure of interest and courtship).

Relax, our person described here in the book will become a scoundrel after the first phrase of acquaintance, then further all this verbal lies will only multiply, and be stored on the shelves of stupidity.

Invisible services – you are engaged in mysticism and magic? Oh, look, the bunny ran, followed by an herbivorous dinosaur. They have love. This bunny will eat all this grass. Don't believe? Take a camera and shoot an adult video, otherwise this rabbit will come to you in a dream and will teach you how to live on.

Starting dating, people present only two scenarios for the development of relationships:
- Serious – for the purpose of creating a family.
- Entertaining – in order to get beautiful memories and psychophysical relax.

Such a contrasting barrier greatly hinders taking a make the first step towards acquaintance. Everyone wants entertainment, games, and beautiful memories. Even those people who want to create a family are forced to play by the rules of dating, that are they understand that will look strange from the outside if their thoughts the keep straightforward. It sounds harsh and scares off those who want to get acquainted. Therefore, they have to choose an entertaining scenario for the development of relationships, which is absolutely unacceptable for them. But those who want to get acquainted with the purpose of entertainment, on the contrary, deliberately try to involve new participants in their environment from those who have not yet decided what they are looking for in life or from those who want to create a family, but them are deceived into believing that in the future everything will be like this they see and want.

There are many hidden things in partnerships. Are you sure that you are happy and there are no secrets? Congratulations, you have become a winner among the members of the club «A lot of fairy tales from the most obedient and trusting»

The moment of the first meeting, this is something incredible, strong, curious, enchanted, and alluring. Subsequently, the words will change to unintelligible abuse and statements that it was a hoax; that this choice was the grandest mistake of a lifetime, etc. So who is lying to whom and who is deceiving?

It is very rare when both partners can say that they fell in love from the first time (look). Usually only one of them falls in love like that. He will have to go through the stage of transformation of his habits, interests, beliefs, and so on; he will be forced to love everything that his object of love is interested in. This is in the load between cases, let's say a slight shock. A partner without much love will check the frankness of feelings with the help of a mass of far-fetched tests, and search for the ultimate strength of an individual who in love with him.

Our hero no longer has time to improvise; all this jazz takes the form of a circus performance to the delight of an barely familiar to him audience. Someone from the crowd notices that something is not right, and now appears the first care directed at the boyfriend.

Funny modern life has led us to the statement – if there are beautiful people, and then there are no other people. You cannot say otherwise. A beautiful person is walking down the street, beautiful passengers are sitting on the bus, and the whole world is very beautiful. Don't laugh, there's no cheating here. Why do you distrust these words? Does it amuse you, intrigue, and make you laugh? Then why do all of us beautiful people offer so many beauty services? To be even more beautiful, simplies transcendent beauty all over the world! And we are ready to meet and get acquainted with this beauty. We try the first time, the second, and the third and so on. There is a lot of beauty, but there is no result. Is something else needed? Of course! People need sexuality, mysticism and inexplicable energy that makes you enthrall into other worlds. A man from another world full of secrets and legends is interesting. But just a partner from the house opposite is boring, and we do not notice him. Blame in this, your childhood habits of eating candy, and reading bedtime stories.

Maybe this rule is laid down by our instinct – to look for partners with a new set of genes to continue healthy offspring? If, however, the love of sweets has been preserved, then your instinct is money! Little advice! Put a piggy bank on your desktop, each thrown coin, its sound will cause you and your client to have an easy orgasm. Learn to get money, it's very sexy.

Those who love intricate scenarios; this is what they live for. Look at your official undersign in the document – pride, the path to success and glory! Don't worry if the computer system sets this field to null. You haven't been erased yet! This is the surprise you've been waiting for a long time. Invisible services surround the object of love and no one promised that everything would be positive. Mysticism is what dating is. Have you ever heard stories about how people after meeting lost laughter, joy, luck, health, life? Fasten your seat belts mortals; it's time to go somewhere.

The place is fashionable and very evil – it is called pure logic. Try not to think otherwise, your every thought will generate many open questions.

We simulate the situation: You think that you are initiating acquaintances in order to find a couple: for living together; parasitism; or for spending a good time? No. You are just a set of information trail seeking to experience with the help of your future partner the expected states and the intrigues of unpredictable events. Why do you need it? Logic ends your existence, you are dead. Logic will never give you the opportunity to enjoy something big, beautiful. Logic optimises all life and strives to stop it. Logic will never give an opportunity to develop the theme of the meaning of life, unpredictability and in general. In it model cannot exist the incomprehensible and unconscious.

By the way, our whole life and the worlds around us are just incomprehensible and unconscious. Therefore, our desire to find a partner to lies (consist of) in a simple escape from our lonely logical thoughts, which, in monologues and our own reflections, absorb and kill us. Therefore, people are not able to find the meaning of life, because to solve this problem they use only logical thinking! Hello, this is Paradox.

You noticed that discussions about the search for the meaning of life tend to go beyond the number of participants. This is people driven by logic require and seek for an exact answer in their strict system. Of course, they are not able to know this, if even the number of participants in the discussion to increase. It's hard to imagine if there are other mindset among people not related to logic, and if so, how to use it? Maybe, all each of us has something that compensates or takes over some of the functions, providing us with something about that is hard for us to guess? Intuition, flair, mysticism!

Let describe below a common practical model of thinking of a lonely person.

So, people grow up, it's time to think about the meaning of life. A lonely person thinks about how to spend the day, his thoughts rest on the fact that he is lonely, he is bored and wants something like not understandable, he thinks about the meaning of life – that is, about dating!

The logic of the individual does not find an answer to this question and requires outside help. The individual has to fight his obsessive logical thinking by finding a partner. After finding a partner, the question of the meaning of life should cease to exist because this is the answer – you found what you were looking for – a partner, this is the meaning of life.

It's very simple – but people don't see it!

You noticed your own state when thoughts want or demand to find a partner, and when a partner was found, your logic still sought to ask him a question about the meaning of life. And in principle, it was didn't matter to you what the answer would be, because your logical thinking in advance asked a lot of questions close to your life aspiration. At the time of the question about the meaning of life, you already knew exactly the answer of your partner. Therefore, you were need a same process of finding a partner, and just a few words – an attempt to answer this question. After finding a partner and his incomplete answer to the question, your early needs to find the answer will be stopped, ceases to exist. That is why the meaning of life is dating.

Our example described above is relevant for those who are looking for or have been looking for the meaning of life. Those who live without limiting themselves and own thinking within the framework of logic does not need such reflections and arguments. They enjoy life and creativity. For them, it just doesn't exist any meaning of life.

This means that it is possible to get out of the obsessive state – a logical (computer) person and become just a moral and sensual person. Don't buy flowers because logic says, I'm invited to the party and should buy flowers. Buy flowers because you want to give flowers a loved one.

Here is the answer, why people who are looking for an answer to the question of the meaning of life are not so interesting for dating. They are very logical and closed from feelings.

All that will be happens next from the meaning of life – is the search for happiness.

Close Extremes to Love

The society of the lonely and the society of the family, if you had a reaction speed like that of a hummingbird, then it would be possible to predict the actions of others at the initial stage of their formation, but it would not bring happiness because logic does not make mistakes, and if there are no mistakes, then there is no need to correct them. If you have nothing to fix, you lose happiness.

Happiness is when you have the opportunity to correct your actions, deeds, attitudes towards someone or something. That is why logically thinking persons are unhappy, they are not up to happiness, and their thinking requires accurate answers and executions. Need to be flexible and capable of dialogue and concessions as a person, then you can get closer to happiness.

Emotions are another very unstable place where it is better not to linger for a long time. When people are meeting, among them there is no psycho–logical state. At such moments they do not correspond to their type of behaviour. The body does not obey the logic of thought, speech turns into a primitive short text, pleasure changes to stress, sexuality increases trying to straighten out a funny situation. A spectacular turn and a clumsy gait complete the job. Now, you can sit down at your table and let off steam. Congratulations, you are acquainting. Now, you can call all contacts and tell how cool you are. Delight!

Unfortunately, in such acquaintances, is often used doping

– alcohol or something else that helps to reduce or equalise the intellectual abilities of those who want to get acquainted. This is just one of the radical ways to cope with the problem of choosing a partner, about which wrote Sigmund Freud. So, dinosaurs exist, live inside us and require sacrifice. This is the way to go for a one-night stand.

Do you think they are capable of love? These are illusions; name at least one reason why a human should be kind. He is omnivorous, enough smart, cunning, able to pretend, rival.

We warned above in the text, that our person described in the book at the first word of acquaintance becomes a scoundrel. Think well, before or during the process of dating, a person in love (or not in love) notices his guilt for involving the chosen object in psychophysical experiences, and strive to quickly disguise own actions with the help of a scenario for creating a romantic development relationship.

A kind, sympathetic and sincere person will not agree with our opinion, his remark will be as follows: «A lover never notices his guilt about initiating an acquaintance.» Then the question is, what causes the behaviour of care, attention, and introduction? You recognise that one person requires or wants something from another person. You think that the lover has love and is ready to share love. It is not right. Love is a whole feeling that comes to life not on the pages of a book or somewhere in a box with a gift, but directly in a person. It is not possible to perform any kind act of transferring love or part of it to another person. In another way, we can say that the love of one person is not enough for two. It is possible to come to reciprocity in good feelings only from the position of enrichment, and not division. Why make yourself miserable, weak, boring; cause such behaviour in a partner a feeling of anxiety. All this will initially lead to simple care, and then if it continues regularly, then to the loss of love.

Zick Rubin, a USA, psychologist, many years ago, he proposed three starting-basic elements with the help of which is formed the feeling of love: *Attachment*; *Caring*; *Intimacy*. What can we say, written kindly and not about love.

Attachment – the desire for the physical presence of a loved one and the willingness to receive/show emotional support.

Many people live close together every day and even receive and show emotional support, but alas, they do not have love.

Caring – concern and action to ensure the welfare of another.

We live together and love each other for the sake of caring – sounds stupid, degrading; mutually provokes to laziness; takes away the desire to be an active person. Honey, let me help you tie your shoelaces. «It is better to do everything yourself than to live in care» – said the failed fictional Emperor.

Earlier in this book, we wrote that criticism (care) from a loving person to the object of love is perceived by him sharply and negatively. We tried to develop a controversy on this issue: Why is the object of love negative to remarks; what is wrong with this if a loving person wants to suggest, correct some aspects of his partner. So, because love between adults is not a care, it is the ability to enrich, endow each other with super-abilities. If one of the partners refuses to upgrade the physical or virtual, then love disappears and appears verbal bullying (weak, simple, boring, and so on). Of course, no each partner will refuse a free beneficial upgrade (care), for example, in the form of a desired gift, money, a compliment and praise for something. But when care turns towards efforts on oneself, then the individual refuses such enrichment and super-abilities. He retreats in search of comfort, why strain for love? It is better to watch TV, while sitting on the sofa.

Example! Imagine my husband can do everything; he has golden hands and a smart head. He takes on any job for me and our love. I admire him. He speaks that glad to work and doing it not difficult.

Our verdict is that – he will not be able to make a love. Business trips, a busy work schedule, separation, and most importantly, not understanding that praise, idealization and obtaining super-abilities should proceed mutually, otherwise to arise an imbalance between the abilities of partners. Modeling this situation shows us that the imbalance between the acquired abilities (new skills) will inevitably lead the relationship into a boring care aimed at lagging behind in development a partner, plunging a bright feeling of love into the shadows.

You are loved, cared for, but you realise that you are not able to do what easily doing others. The emotional state goes into a negative; you are depressed and in your eyes appear sadness. You have been deprived of the opportunity to be useful not only because you are beauty, but also because you are actually not able to keep up with the modern world, as well physically, intellectually and morally.

People themselves long time ago answered on many questions, obvious that care between adults – is not love, and not even a part. Than do people think when they try to share love between themselves for personal purposes; or into parts for scientific analysis? Please give the tastiest piece to me!

Modern man in terms of thinking about love did not go far in development from the man of ancient, who at one time met the new and the unknown with the helping of taste. And now, among a human with love same thing happens, the ancient instinct requires to bite love, and while the teeth are doing their job, the eyes will carefully look at the bitten off piece of love, allowing the brain to better analyse the composition of this delicacy. *Mmm*, what did they put in there? Delicious, nutritious, I like it, wait, I ate my partner!

How do you think, why we are a little higher in the text list the abilities of human development in separate words: «…as well physically, intellectually and morally» Life experience tells us that people are not able to fully conform to intellectual behaviour, even partially beneficial to them. Having a set of built-in mechanisms governing moral behaviour, a person will perform actions characteristic of his own initiative, and not the one that circumstances require. Morality is an intellectual struggle of logic with a continuous psychedelic, both, as internal and external, surrounding the individual our entire imperfect world.

It is known that not every person of high moral culture can rebuild own psychological behaviour in the direction of low morality. This incapacity is caused by work, including also the highest priorities of thinking, which block the actions of the individual or the critical choice between life and death. Entering into a stupor or a nervous failure triggers a cycle of indifference, which is an incorrect logical decision leading to the answer: «I can't do it» (situations: being in love; love; protecting the name and dignity; family; property; requests; services and actions, including unfaithfulness, etc.)

Let's look at a few examples:
- The partner wants to film sex scenes – the answer of the moral partner will be: «I can't do this» and «I don't want to lose this partner because in everything else we are very similar and we have no other disagreements. » – Stupor, consent, motor,

camera, filmed!

- To my house entered unknown persons, they threaten the lives of me and my wife. I have only two patrons and there are four of them. I must to shoot, but then I can kill someone. «I cannot do this.» – Suicidal thoughts.
- I liked one person and I want to sleep with him, but this will mean unfaithfulness. «I cannot do this.» – Nervous failure. In this example, a highly moral person not is such, therefore after some time... (Do you often think so dirty?)

In principle, society it is time to admit the fact that highly moral people simply not exist. Time to time people go down even lower than it is possible to imagine, someone in their thoughts, and someone else physically. If you are firmly stranded, then make your feet from the company in which you find yourself. Don't delay choosing, ask a big whale to take you on the shore, while from you didn't make a boat.

Especially, for suspicious people, we will write that there are no hopeless situations in life. If you are on the verge of a nervous failure or experiencing psychological abuse, ask for support, calm down. Believe us, our whole life is a movement similar to a marathon in which and participants and spectators run looking at each other without seeing a cliff ahead. It's tragic. You all remember: «Someone being in love at the moment when were untied the laces, and someone at that moment when the wig was twisted to the side.»

Try to show care for loved on a treadmill, well, at least tell how much you love him: «I, I, I, love, you, very much!»

Here in these words we would like to focus on. When people show care, then of course, they follow words declaration of love. Do you think a person in love has that a right, and should that person apologise for such behave, especial if this to case someone hurt?

We believe it is imperative to apologise, restrained and with dignity. The psyche of people works with undulating periods of mood swings and therefore sometimes it is necessary to apologise twice, at the moment and after some time.

Being in love is a game of zombies – they not only want to get to know you, but also to touch and infect you. The difficulty of this game lies in how to recognise the right partner, who nevertheless admits that he, has immersed the idea of love in you. This is necessary for the realization of your revenge, verbal-sensual, material, psychophysical. For example, when you were infected with a cold, are you ready to rejoice at this event and for the person who did it? Most likely: No. There are activated scenario of revenge, which manifests itself brighter in difficult life moments, in fact being a punishment and a little later care (primarily for oneself), since the brain will receive signals about the salvation of the tormented body in which it is located. Haven't you noticed that it is the brain that more often wants to get a new body endowed with beauty, strength and endurance? Therefore, we adhere to the principle that one-sided being in love is – guilt for an act, punishment, and further care arising from the process of fooling and punishing. You were deceived and forced to participate in this stupid game. This is not love; this is a simple algorithm for your protection. But, the mutual being in love that synchronously arose in a couple of people is love. They have nothing to apologise for in such a situation, they are lucky! Congratulations!

Love in the memory of our brain consists of memories and expectations. Try to keep your attention on the present tense and you will understand that it simply does not exist in the theoretical model of love. For that to feeling love in the present, you need to provide a special moment: being in love, theater, starry sky, a walk to the door of the house, thoughts about desire. So, what happened to you? Or it hasn't happened yet. You were in an exceptional moment, the present belonged to you. Why do scientists claim that after three years being in love disappears, and love vanishes in the present tense, turning into care? Maybe love is not an intimate, but a social feeling? Of course, is not.

Intimacy – close trusting relationship. Partners freely share thoughts, ideas, experiences among themselves, feel support.

In this form «*Intimacy*» – it's just friendly relationship. Moreover, when are speaking about friendship, most often mean the fidelity necessary for partners, teams, that is, people involved in some kind of responsible work. But, love isn't a work. If for me personally to indicate that love is – a business, then I will not participate in this business because all life is a continuous business.

Please note, that being in love is more often incipient not from old friendships, but from a random new event – attraction, therefore it is very doubtful to assume that later people will value love as a concept such as friendship. Hi, friend!

All these three basic elements of love seem to have been identified by a specialist at the stage of development of romantic relationships. If you remember, in our understanding, a person in love is that person who initiates an acquaintance, and involves a third-party person in his psychophysical problem (concern, interest, sex, being in love, love.) That is why we believe it is not correct to claim that A*ttachment*; C*aring*; *Intimacy* are the basic elements of love. Who knows the true motives of such a desire? A person experiences several feelings at the same time: being in love, his own benefit, or something else. Maybe, he earlier stole something from the object of love, and then also fell in love? In, as much as, there are no pure relationships.

What would to learn to understand the interest processes, it is necessary to see, that is, to have the initial data before the upcoming event, then the data of the process itself and its result. Do you think we will do this with love? Easy, because love for many people is a deception and punishment, therefore to they need our attention and support.

Does anyone know what is the meaning of the common statement; «In love you must be faithful,» if you were fooled at the very beginning of your acquaintance (being in love). To forgive! Is this really the most important element of human thinking and character, allowing you to feel or find happiness, because you could, helped or tried to fix something?

Based on the understanding that usually people do not fall in love with each other at the same time, and in such a scenario they apparently have deception and punishment in a relationship, and then let's ask ourselves: are there other options that are closer and tend to reciprocity?

For example, maybe people are better off first try to get acquainted with good intentions for a simple friendship, and only then after a while look at each other and fall in love? But here, too, being in love sticks out of friendly pants with an asynchronous action.

So, how can two single people fall in love at one moment, at first sight and find reciprocity through a third party or through the bartender?

No, he does not need such happiness. Why then listen your complaints and scandals?

Turn on your brain, love at first sight exists, but sometimes it leads to a dramatic plot. Do not fly in the clouds, in front of you is located not just a person, but a whole mystery. How do you have so much confidence that the chosen object of love is the expected person for your criteria of selection? Do you understand that you are deceiving yourself? Gambling game is a game to stake one's all!

Please explain to us why you choose risky behaviour, being a reasonable and moral person. Do you want to quickly pick up problems, and then solve and fix them in order to find happiness?

Well, actually, we don't quite represent happiness in this way, although according to our description above, there is no error in the text. We probably need to provide a detailed answer regarding the fact that happiness is – when you have the opportunity to correct your own mistakes, because if you correct all the mistakes, then you will lose happiness, and if you intentionally or accidentally multiply mistakes, then you will also lose happiness, because you will not have time to enjoy your result (what happiness is it to endlessly correct your mistakes?).

Funny! Therefore, you yourself will have to regulate the level of truth/lies in matters of finding a partner. This is your need and blames only yourself for all this, not forgetting to apologise to those who were overtaken by your desire to acquaint.

Well, let's continue on. Do you think love is a pleasant deceit? Imagine how many high-quality emotions you can experience if you together plunge into a difficult relationship. It's very tempting. Who can resist front a beautiful figure, a mysterious look, rich in imagination. You will feel the triumph of our thought, but you are in the future will certainly want to immerse in your partner frank idea expressed in an intimate relationship, for example, invite him to a jacuzzi or force to do something improbable, which at the moment seems impossible. Do you think we are destroying the foundations of cultural education? No. We create the prerequisites for the realization that there are things that require your attention.

The functioning of our body is the priority of the brain. As much as we don't want to go beyond the psychophysical capabilities, we must understand that acquaintance with person who has significant differences from your characteristics is a behaviour that defies many established rules. You are loved to crush and break?

Then apparently you initially, even before love, want to punish yourself, your «soul» and body for some kind of offense – try to guess for yourself, and we will give you a hint: you have not a desire or ability to deceive others.

Imagine such honesty will surely lead people to a close union like that of a giraffe and a turtle. Of course, the person is feels that all case in him, because the others it is somehow easy to get acquaint and find a partner: approached, smiled, greeted, enthrall.

An honest person studying this simple algorithm is not able to fully understand what the meaning is and what is interesting in this algorithm in order to find a partner. Thinking people will argue for a long time, complicate and invest even more exotic judgments from the point of view of logic. Not finding with own minds clues, they for completing this logical thinking, will choose a partner that differs from themselves, at least in physical parametres. What for?

Answer: They are smarter than us.

Rest assured, when we work for you, superfluous psychology is discarded, here there is no time for tenderness, people themselves reveal their secrets and want that others to stare at them.

Incompatibility exists only in conjunction with a quality quiet life, in other cases, when an extraordinary couple faces with trials, versatile skills and abilities are better suited to overcome crises.

Now, the most interesting, how do you think, are there many couples who, let's face it, consider themselves compatible or partially compatible – probably such couples do not exist. And therefore, we will build our defence based on the assertion that incompatibility is the reality of our world, consequently, in order to personal relationships to gain a goal, people use or invent crises in order to feel the ability to overcome them.

You will say that's what everyone says. And you can name the main aspiration of this activity?

Really, and here need to make a hint: People will aspire to create crises and in the process of solving them get feelings of compatibility – this is the only scarce element in personal relationships (in bunch with a quiet life).

Even also and sex requires building diversity, in order to appear the ability to unite (increasing the feeling of compatibility).

How often do people need to exchange partners? The answer is obvious, every time. It's the same as cooking or being a musician. We are programmed to constantly change. For example in sex cannot be reiteration, even both regular partners each time will experience absolutely different sensations. Thoughts can, of course, be approach to the analogy of past experience (for example some people have the same dreams), but still it every time is something new.

Please to think; in sex there are two ways of psychological «pleasure»

- Punishing a partner – in this case is achieved the main goal integration with purpose to obtain a sense of compatibility. Permanent partners need to achieve this comfort in a relationship by almost any methods; the need to focus on the so that the couple does not break up. When punishing a partner, the active partner will think only about the object of punishment, and the other partner, experiencing punishment will think about the active partner. Don't worry, they know how to play on feelings by changing roles;
- New – achievable only with the help of unfaithfulness. If we are talking about permanent partners (married couple), then by unfaithfulness we will understand not so much physical, but more semantic relationships. Examples: Partner unilaterally decides to indulge in solitary sex, possibly with of multimedia, sex toys and the like – unfaithfulness; Partners usually strive to create tender romantic mood, implying sex based on trust or fidelity. And this is yet another deception. That in single or mutual sex, partners can let their imaginations to fly free, where there are will be presence intriguing plots of unfaithfulness. The most resilient people will brush off from exotic thoughts in own minds with the help of punishment, for example, directed first of all at themselves (to focus attention and confirm fidelity).

Tricky! You know, the topic of sex is always unfaithfulness. In it there is no permanent partner, there are only stupid thoughts striving to be funny.

New – deceit (unfaithfulness) and punishment (maybe in the form of unfaithfulness) moves people. We wonder how else you can imagine punishment between adults. What other meaning should be used for whether to feel compatibility, unification, to get a partner in oneself hands.

Pat on the shoulder, and say I understand you? No.

In partnerships, the most important thing is to keep the partner. Each of us is constantly looking for motivational tools so that deception does not destroy us.

People, in principle, should not worry about the topic of unfaithfulness. Count how many lies throughout the day will be registry your eyes, ears and mind. Given this fact, it becomes obvious that the person involved in partnerships necessarily choose an only that motivational strategy such as punishment. This is the same vector of development of relations.

Of course, we know quite a few kind people who value relationships built on trust and fidelity. Perhaps, they in the past made some mistake, gained negative experience or perceive that it is better to live in love and care. But this is illusions; in fact, these people are experiencing a deficit of lies and punishment. Of course, everyone knows that evil is bad, but who is claims that this hidden need, beckoning to wild places, where a dense forest turns a person into a frightened, gentle, obedient creature ready for joint activity, must certainly be realised. Whose is this initiative, please come to the mirror.

Let's ask some chaos, and provocative questions:
- What is the point of demanding fidelity – so that you are not deceived?
- Are you going to deceive?
- Why are you afraid of deception? Are you feeling yourself weak?
- Do you dislike punishment, or are you unable to punish others?

- For what offense do partner want to punish you? Will you give answer or will you be the initiator of punishment for the guilty person?
- Even a person with an impeccable reputation can find in such a situation, and then why be afraid of all this?
- Keeping a partner – is it your meaning?
- Are you able to apologise for your mistakes or forgive your offender?

In order to collect this whole puzzle «plus twenty one» you will need: quill pen, chair, silk ribbon and one tasty partner. Interesting what he keeps in his head, going to love you?

Find a partner. If you look at the topic of finding a partner, then we can say that people do this with the help of attraction, which in turn covers many areas of human knowledge: socio-cultural, genetics, psychology, hormonal and pheromone medicine, chemistry.

From this entire list, it is better to read the astrological forecast and begin to operate. You know that adults are not given advice on the topic of love; even best friends do not have the right to advise you. By the way, this book was written not for science, but for getting emotions. We do not doubt your abilities and we are sure that you will be finding a partner by the evening.

Already was found!

So, we look. – Beautiful!

Wait, why do you have orange hair and a fake red nose? You fooled us – this is a photo from a fashion magazine.

Okay – Respect!

Now, let's move on to practice, we also played a prank on you, in one day you can only find a fashion magazine. Scroll through it; think about what meaning you want to invest in an acquaintance. For example, how do you want to enter the history of future relationships, with the help of a riddle, romance, business style or provincial? Maybe, you also are not from this planet, and then we will wait for our spaceship.

Love at first sight is a cocktail consisting of rapacity, risk, delight, beauty and intelligence. After such a meeting, you will remember in detail only the nose, some forms of body and the height of the object of love. Even the colour of the eyes is unlikely to be remembered, although at that exceptional moment you seemed to drown in them. Black colour!

What to do if it was just a moment and thoughts still do not go away? Probably, this is not the case. Forget it. Do you know how many such looks can be seen in a few days? Stop. Rip out this page of the book and tear it to shreds, we are lying.

Our words have no effect on you. Let's explain why. At that moment, you liked something completely others. The human essence does not consist of good deeds, but such as: to hunt, to track down your victim. Meeting eyes is a challenge addressed to the evolutionary development of living beings. The line between like and being in love/love is not significant to vision and the brain, which interprets visual signal «like» and distributes that meaning into your matrix – templates of similar experience. For example, you like morning fishing, or vice versa, you prefer to sleep longer, read a favourite book, take a walk in nature, eat at a restaurant, repair a bike, watch a movie, shoot at a shooting range, and so on. Probably we should not continue the thought about who likes what, this value contains several meanings, and it is not known yet for what purposes – good or evil.

Look, here on the bench sitting embittered lovers, them like it! They are trying to reach a deficient psychological state of compatibility by creating some problems. If they have a «money box» of meanings in a relationship, then they will be a couple for many years. If in meaning will be laid limited essences or generally incorrectly matched, then the couple will experience a deficit of compatibility, which reduces the level of comfort and causes more anger. This behaviour does not mean that their relationship will end in the shortest possible time, but rather the «friction» of incompatibility will be eliminated by scandals, legal intimidation or other force. Having sunk to the bottom and lost a lot of health, they will begin a constructive dialogue or admit their fiasco.

Why something inside us demands to make a hasty choice. From the side, you can see when an unrealised idea more and more eats into the brain. The desire to get this particular person passes from the stage of being in love and love, into physical attraction. The first tactful conversations after a while turn into the plane of consumption – using stronger words; lovers release sexual energy and strive to accumulate more positive feelings. As soon as, their thoughts and meanings are revealed to them, the relationship will become more informal; partners will begin to notice a deficit of compatibility, surface emotional swings.

Us don't care this. Not normative words – destroy. Ashamed to admit, but sometimes a caustic word causes delight and a storm of emotions, though this is extremely uncultured. What to do if an individual, for example, has a difficult day and needs psychological relief. Do you want to limit him? Learn other words, translate them into more intriguing, ones that are easy for learn. Important to follow the etiquette and have development of relationship.

In love, any words are a striving for compatibility, so they should be taken as levels of compatibility. Dialogue may be a theatrical game, sometimes as an assistant, sometimes as an experienced specialist. Do not argue, and do not repeat many times about the same thing, you need to do what your partner wants, he has the right to make mistakes in order to correct them later... «Getting happiness» Remember, when you are asked to do something, it most likely means that you are given the opportunity to become the initiator of the case – an active performer.

People do not know how to unite and appreciate the feeling of compatibility in an ordinary comfortable life. We personally do not know such persons who, being at home, show interest in each other. Maybe, of course, there are partners whose level of lovingness allows, say, to take care of their health, but most often, before sex couples tend to use negative stimulus (smoking, drinking, watching adult videos, etc.) in order to cause attraction.

Positive stimulus and sex are incompatible concepts. At least fifty per cent of partners (funny guess) do not get enjoyment from romantic evenings, considering them too cloying and boring for the release of sexual energy.

In principle, a romantic evening with an alcoholic menu (that harmful for health) is not a positive stimulus, but due to the fact that it is in itself a historical tradition, a classic of relationships, so the topic of sexuality, greatly fades into the background, causing related feelings between love, care, morality, responsibility, obligations, and even something entirely social. Try to have sex, keeping such a list in your head – more precisely in your hand, where can you find at least thirteen centimetres of romance here?

Couples in love for full the feeling of compatibility, it is necessary to regularly unite and comment on gained the experience. Therefore, it turns out that only stupid actions assist to relationships. Yes, we wrote above that it is possible to compensate for the feelings of compatibility and also receive this through the process, from some kind of joint work activity, but this is just a small part necessary for a full-fledged relationship. Of course, two people together are able to build a house, get from this a whole lot of different emotions and impressions, but if there is no bed or sofa in the house, this will mean that the relationship is in a crisis. In principle, everything is already obvious, if initially the partners tried to be clever, discuss, procrastinate the topic of love avoiding sexuality and sex, then probably them should not continue such a relationship.

Reincarnation into a human, throughout life, all of us are periodically given the opportunity to take steps towards happiness, well, in any case, it seems to people somewhere like this. And now, let's ask ourselves the question: is the concept of happiness something capable of being achieved, if we take and try to make efforts to find it? Probably, answering on this question should be treated with caution. Without going into details right away, we frankly feel the presence of intersecting interests from different emotional experiences, which clearly makes it difficult to more accurately determine what one strives for, and what one wants to acquire the human desire for happiness.

The first statement can be clarified – that each of us is not in equal conditions and abilities to achieve such a goal. Yes or no?

By the second statement, we must note – that when making certain mistakes and correcting them (in an effort to find happiness), not everyone can feel and understand why this activity is necessary, why it is so important for the individual, and what actually expresses happiness. Based on the logic of this second statement, for us remains only one conclusion – that in order to attract our attention and interest, demand some other mechanism starting the search for new emotional behaviour from which our body and mind will begin to receive benefits (pleasure).

In this there is no speculation, indeed, for some, happiness is an opportunity to correct their mistakes, while for others, happiness is something unknown and which can be reached using a other mechanism of emotional cognition.

As you know, in the striving to happiness there are meanings, for example, expressed by the desire to become famous and rich, smart and successful, beautiful and healthy...

And know, how that all this can classify and organise in head? Perhaps this is important. A person usually does not use only one single meaning, the striving of happiness, and therefore each of us must be able to know, feel and manage entire lists of own meanings of happiness.

The question is, from what consists of happiness? We affirm that happiness consists from emotions. These are all emotions even the desire to be smart is primarily a need to feelings.

Let's offer an example. A person has an average level of education and strives to raise it even higher. What is this? Needs of emotions or logic and mind? Do you think pure logic – the mind requires knowing something? No. Only by turning on the emotional chip in your head can start talking about your own growth and development; without emotionality, our brain and head become useless.

Therefore, it remains to be understood whether there is an

important to experience this feeling (happiness) or is it just another deception, or rather flattery about what you would like to achieve or have.

For example, many people want to reach old age and receive good news about successes from their grown-up children. Suppose, you will be receiving such news, but in reality you do not know anything. It is enough to remember how many successful people have lost or destroyed the best and strongest relationships and more. Or, correcting this example, one can boldly ask why people don't really care what will happen to their great-grandchildren, is a person really not able to think about the future?

Therefore, we strongly do not recommend that you hide behind the concept of happiness, it is not beautiful. People are driven by emotions and nothing more. Happiness in our understanding is emotions, or rather a large set.

The older generation easily finds happiness with the help of the statement – that happiness is when a person can experience various emotions, from neutral and positive to moderately negative. This is the value of knowing our world, the skills gained and further development should be interconnected with a special quality of an individual such as Humanity.

Persons unable to for some reason to adhere to this rule, it would be good to learn to reincarnation again. It's not just some fun ritual or fancy training; it's an effort to stop discord through acts of goodwill. You know, that to become an interesting person, need to learn to forgive. Remember how was terrible to meeting with pure logic, imagine if such a person is next to you. He will be punctual, demanding and not friendly. Is it possible to live comfortably in the world, being under surveillance, total control, continuous bans and reports? No.

Trackers on the wrist, in the bag, in the car, at work and at home, why are they needed if your bank knows almost everything about you. Maybe, in the future, financial companies will take on the role of finding a partner for similar characteristics: income and consumption levels, age, gender, inventory of movable and immovable property.

Then let's learn to lie. If someone being in love to you for real, he will have to forgive and laugh at your lies. This prank will hurt for stupid and straight-thinking people. So what, they must understand that relationships are not methods of optimization, but life.

Yet if there is love, then keeping a partner becomes a priority. How are you going to keep your love? Witchcraft, magic, intelligence, delicious dinner, fun, sex, gifts, fists, nothing, or something else! Yes, it that happens, the universe has an end – emptiness is the end.

Therefore, it is important to invest some interesting meaning at the very beginning of the relationship. Answer to the question: What is the value of the relationship for you?

Answers such as:

*to create a family,

*age requires, otherwise I will be alone forever,

*copying life like friends,

*need an assistant.

Have no value for keeping love (relationships).

Here is listed your desire to change lifestyle, and this is not the meaning of the relationship.

The meaning of relationships is the joint ability to discover other worlds and fill them with life, feelings, beauty. This is not a job, not a requirement and obligation. This is the desire to create a fulfilling life, where your activity is a gift to achieve this. Imagine that you were given a mind, and then a physical brain and body with which you can create, experience emotions, love.

Use your body and mind. Tourism is ideal to suit for dating and developing relationships. Begin with local short excursions, they are beneficial because do not cause overwork. The presence of a guide and the proposed programme of visiting historical sites help to switch from work to leisure. Do not be surprised if ninety per cent of the bus passengers will be older people, seen in the salon two young adults, they certainly them will get engaged (married).

The subject area always has an impact on dating, so first try to think about whom you want to meet; and whether it is possible to achieve this exactly where you are going to go. It's simple; feelings start searching for a pattern, and later provide an answer. The work of logic here will be minimal, emotions will not allow you to miss a bright chance to experience a new risk for achieve pleasure.

Let's go somewhere else one more time.

This time we are going to nature, where the road rises to the mountains and to lie through passes from which our head is spinning. In such places, sheer cliffs have power; they put pressure on the consciousness and displace from people the energy sphere, to remain for itself a timid body for direct dialogue. Time to strive to go faster, the body reproduces the memory of cells and demands to continue the path. The road to dodge and descends into the valley. Is coming an impenetrable night. The driver stops on the side of the road and turns off the engine. We fall into silence. The fog does not allow moving forward. One of us decided to get out of the car to do a warm-up, but his legs seemed to fall into the abyss, there was a splash of water and an interrogative exclamation: «Where does the water come from under the wheels? Just two minutes ago, the ground was dry and hard. Now, we can't come back onto the road, the car is completely stuck in viscous soil. » That's too ordered the nature. It expects something from us, still in the mountains we must to talk with her sincerely.

People think that love is capable of much, but in this place there is no love. No, because nature does not know this feeling, it only a have energy, colossal. A person, who is in the path of energy waves, loses sexual energy and love too. He understands that his significance in such places is equal to nothing. Remember that moment of truth when consciousness accurately calculated your energy and compared it with the energy of nature. It is you who must adjust your body and mind to its laws and regulations in order to try to add forty years of life to your list of dubious pleasures. Do you agree, that many of us to be taken in by this wealth and are ready to start loving everyone for just to stay on this planet too longer. It looks like some kind of gamble, where the main idea is the ability to deceive you. Timid attempts after a while begin to bear fruit. Finding harmony through love, helps connect to the energy of nature. This means that in relationships definitely will be added the love let it make to you pleasant.

So what is love and which feelings do it calling?

Thinking about love, we imagine: tenderness, beauty of the body, phone calls, walks holding hands, delight and awe from the thought that has appeared desired partner, the scent of flowers, warm evenings, first kisses, dreams and plans for the present and future.

Really all this is not enough? Why in beautiful make some additions push and fundamentally argue.

And after these open words, we will try to reach harmonious relations. But first, a question; so, how do you imagine what it is?

Harmony (without radicalism) is the ability to be able to live in the environment in which you are. In any case, a person will adapt to the conditions of life, and not vice versa. For example, ambitious people will not agree with this statement. They will immediately say that in the basic conditions of life there cannot be talk of any harmony, therefore, is needed a lot of money to provide a person with better living conditions. Build a palace, hire servants, to give everything needs and even do more. Only then, is it possible to find harmony. It remains to sympathise with them, they will not find harmony. A person should be friends with the world and with him now, and not dream that this will ever happen even if you work hard and go towards the goal. We believe that an adult person must be able to find a state of harmony throughout the day, otherwise it should be indicated that in this person emotional cognition and feelings are not set up correctly.

Bad things are happening. Harmony can be a very dangerous phenomenon, for example, in the manifestations of human extremes of the concepts of good and evil, a broken psyche and thinking. Of course, we would like that is aspirations people for harmony will be too moderately positive, that is for why we wrote: «a person should be friends with the world and himself in present time…»

The question is which people are more harmonious single or married. This question is not correct. Harmony is a relationship with the world. If at this stage of life you have learned to comfortably interact with a limited range of entities, then the next stage of development can be assumed to be its expansion, but this is not a mandatory rule, but a simple possibility that does not strive for infinity of knowledge to the detriment of someone or something.

In such a description, a person is obliged to come to a harmonious relationship by transforming his ambitions into concessions to his partner. This is nothing more than shifting existing disagreements into a debt box. People have learned to correct this bias with the help of etiquette and a service counter, you to me, I to you. Feelings of love must be able to adjust so that disagreements move to the list of joint cases, then you will get a double benefit, a solution to the problem and a sense of compatibility. If you are currently in a broken relationship, then you need to reset the service counters with the help of win-win options, well, you yourself know what you love to do together.

For life, relationships and love, there is no identical identity of partners. It's a delusion. Two similar personalities will not merge into a single whole, but will develop as two separate worlds. Sameness is love for me, it is narcissism and selfishness, and it is a strongly pronounced closed interest only in one's own world. Probably, it is greed and suspiciousness caused by the discomfort of hypothetical condemnation from the outside, fear of being in the centre of attention of society if partners have differences (distinctive features). Identity is the striving for comfort in relationships because people it seems that similar interests, thinking and behaviour contribute to more harmonious free relationships, but this is not that. Identical people (if such exist) are not of interest to such like themselves, they exactly know what will happen at the present moment. Deprived the diversity of life, they do not receive the development of relationships; they exclude them, protecting themselves from dependences. Of the main stimulus for striving for identical relationships, one can see the search for harmony in love, beauty, independence and efficiency. These are not insignificant life aspirations, but the concept of independence is in no way consistent with the meaning of relationships. Partners will have to choose either a joint relationship, or a break in relations and a long-awaited independence. The striving of similar people for identity can be represented as the first step in the development of relations, where early or later will have to be taken the second step – the recognition that there are no identical people and relationships must be built taking into account this fact.

Cruel or normal! Is there a third step? Of course, yes, only it is taken back to the first step, the fact is that life is cycles, marking time. In psychology, there is a primitive test for intelligence. In a spacious room, ask the subjects to reflect on the problem. Those who will walk in circles and will be the smartest, others are also smart, they are just easily distracted from tasks, there are drawn to visit us on Mars.

Emotions predetermined human development, for someone to helping or someone is distracted. We won't think about it too long. We have a great mood; there is happiness, harmony, being in love and love.

Mysticism and inexplicable energy go against common sense. Few people believe that a person is a battery and an energy generator, but no matter how much one would like to identify the living world with technical terms, it turns out that there is some truth in this. And from this truth depends our behaviour. There are people who are more likely to feed their energy at the expense of others, you think this is not possible and this cannot be proven. And we are not going to prove anything; we do not live according to the laws of logic, but according to the laws of emotions and feelings. So, if a person feels that he is somehow unusually quickly losing his energy, why should he prove something to others? For example, people long time ago came up with a stupid rule, that silence – means consent, and this rule use more strong persons in relation to the weaker ones, knowing that the latter do not have the strength to justify and defend from the accuser. Therefore, in this world one cannot talk about the truth as seriously as some try to promote it.

People feel the substitution instantly, so it was in ancient times, this is happening and now – this is coercion from which are destroyed meanings, happiness and dreams.

What is left in the ruined world? Show a little attention to ordinary things and you will be shocked, for example, white bathroom ceramics are called by human names.

Our imperfect world is moving away from the model of respect and mutual understanding because society has not learned how to take the first, second and third steps in free relationships. Having united into one big noisy lump, people only need to find a leader capable of generating wisdom – to suggest the direction from which slope of the mountain it is better to roll down.

The search for a leader in a micro relationship, having in mind the relationship between two partners, love will flaunt as a leader. It is so attractive to them, that to lose this feeling becomes consciously stupid. This is the first merit of logic over feelings, or yet we understand with a «round bone» that a person must be moral and therefore love is necessary for all of us.

Another question is why emotions and feelings often require destruction instead of creation. Recharging and spending energy, we pursue the only goal is to register emotions and feelings. When occurs destruction, it means that the individual wishes to test emotions and feelings using various methods of analysis – destruction. Only on condition to break something, you can find out from what it was made, what is inside and how it works. Probably, many of us have experienced on one how cool it is to break love by letting steam out of ears. This enthusiasm is contagious. There are whole groups of lovers of broken relationships and love. Of course, they never intended to break love, on the contrary, they wanted a better relationship from a partner, and overdid it. You know, when a person breaks his love, he actually breaks his head and gets a terrible result – rejection of the relationship. It's almost like demagnetizing sexuality and living in betrayal of your body, deny the necessary natural needs. So, interest must be directed to knowledge through love, but not analysis. For example, I love my partner and I'm not going to break our relationship. Or, I love our big world and I won't spoil it.

It is possible to do this, or rather, it must be done every time, because the world of emotions requires constantly adjustment of feelings. All people live every day in their original way and will never live according to the instructions from the textbook. Someone consciously slows down, and someone is in a hurry to have time to do everything, and even lie down in a coffin. Well done, it's nice to see how fast we move in space. By burning non-renewable resources, the planet Earth becomes lighter; therefore the gravity of the Sun star changes the orbit, warming up the temperament of people and changing habitual behaviour to a new one.

Talking about the present and the future is visible only destruction. That technology, that the strivings of managers, that the economy and rising prices – all point to a transition for restrictions. You feel how interest disappears from such very real perspectives. Therefore, people do not need to give up of relationships, love will to help fix the situation. Of course, we will not be able to return the Earth's orbit, but to rush to break everything and go into oblivion it is not ethical.

Fifty-fifty, such is the chance to find a partner. There are no dead ends in life, acquaintances it is customary to create with the help of even frank conversations or in the form of a riddle, a game with a lot of fantasy that fools and intrigues the participant. Boring or fun, scary or hopeless, no one knows where you are will bring, following for your needs of emotions. The dark side of happiness is just not an opportunity to correct some past event, including those involved in acquaintance. Sometimes, people go ahead of the development of relationships and do not understand that doing so is wrong and not natural. Let's give a classic example from the world of computer games. More than twenty years ago, the developers of a popular online game decided to make a complex algorithm for the interaction of objects in the surrounding world. During the beta testing, they got disappointed, their work was in vain, the players destroyed these objects at such a speed that the algorithm simply had nothing to operate and it was removed from the game.

The speed of thinking and the rhythm of life are different for everyone. If partners have these differences, then it will not be easy for one of them to find harmony. Let's pass this place quickly, for some reason you don't want to stand in line – this is the only condition for finding harmony, suitable for both fast and slow people, none of them likes to stand in line.

Wrong questions, answers and more the other affects the

success of finding a partner. Thinking about the providence of fate and the efforts made, do not worry about a weak result. People have magnetism and sooner or later everything it will work out. Such a generated number of thoughts will open the mind not only of yours, but also of those who are of interest to you. The main thing is not to rush events, otherwise will surface a Turbo-love. Try to guess what it is. This is a holiday romance. Can you do this every day? Then you are in a professional topic, if not, and then you have an evil (revenge) towards yourself or someone from your inner circle. Therefore, we wrote earlier that kind people want punishment, they just cannot directly realise it, but their body tells them and does it.

Strange, does good attract evil? Perhaps, it would be more accurate to say evil attracts evil. And we do not have an answer to this funny question, we pass it from hand to hand for careful storage.

Receding feelings! Having an idea from various sources about how dangerous emotions can be people still underestimate their own capabilities. Before starting a relationship, as they say, you first need to learn how to get out of confusing and difficult situations, and for this you need to read a lot of fiction and special literature, increasing the level of knowledge and developing the ability of the psyche to withstand negative events. Use the rule stating that there are no ideal relationships, therefore, sooner or later disagreements will be overtaken and you can prepare for this in advance. Shall we remove the glassware? Practical, but not enough, you need lessons in hand-to-hand combat skills. Another joke! Teaching you to a reflex response to a threat will lead the body to automaticity of actions, one wrong word and death to a liar will be provided with lightning speed. This happens and no one is immune from bad events. If our words of warning have affected you, then let's turn to psychology, and try to never provoke ourselves and others to aggression. Get to know yourself, think about for which as actions you are ready to break off relations at once. Then, imagine what emotions you will experience. By the way, we will not give advice on this subject, and we also do not want to be witnesses. Personal affairs require respect.

So, conflicts. Finally, appeared a revival of emotions, finally, someone was tired of the current state of affairs, and the mind requires a general cleaning. Nerves were exposed, testosterone made the blood boil; the body acquired a stable posture to scream. Funny, let's ask the first question.

Do you want to teach or punish your partner? It will not work to push everything into his head at once, he is not capable – you yourself that decided, after living together some number of days, or maybe years. So, we look, the cart is rolling along the pavement right at the still smiling friend in misfortune. He thinks that he will jump over it, but the weakness of his legs from the resulting stress knocked him down, ugh delicious jam is ready.

Excuse me, where is the scene of learning? Please call us a screenwriter, and bring ice to the stuntman. We will do a second take in an hour. Let's go, motor, filmed, stop! Why is someone's ass in the frame? The cameraman where is our video track, enough to show your stormy weekend to the entire film team. Please the focus on the details otherwise the audience will not see the real acting of the actors.

Let's continue, as you know, to scandals usually leads the situation of chronic ignoring the comments made earlier. What do you propose to do: break off relations, teach, retrain, and teach a lesson? That resolve this issue, we need to fly in

Australia to the natives and ask for help in mastering the skill of throwing a boomerang. This is a flying club-propeller that is thrown at the victim, and if the target is hit, then the boomerang does not return by inertia to the hunter, and if there was a miss, then the boomerang effectively describes a turn in the air and goes back to where it was launched from – this is theoretical. On practice all you have to do is this, remember?... Go to the store, buy food and cook dinner at home. Scandal is a theater of antics, a test of the ability to gain independence if is not possible to interact together showing the desired effectiveness. Sex, gambling addiction, money, alcohol, smoking, unfaithfulness, ignoring, and so on! – These are the topics from which it is impossible to get away without drastic actions. There are also more petty problems that provoke conversations in raised tones: forgetfulness, night snoring, draught, smells, noise, goes on etc.

Lingering here or dropping a level lower, we physically begin to feel an increasing load on the entire body; our psyche begins to demand a way out of the accumulated discomfort with the help of independence. The algorithm is simple, get up and leave, but since a person has emotionally dependent thinking, that his actions are predetermined by eloquent speech, a monologue. Transformation to speaker is a manifestation of leadership abilities. One of them is tired of living in a ruined world, and in order to create, he must again like his partner. But in this presentation, criticism or directed care is of no interest to the listener because he needs love, food and sex.

If you want a memorable scandal, take off your clothes and talk. It's weak to do this, so, you have greed and unreasonable claims against your partner? What are you trying to hide? You know, there are a lot of pleasant psychological tricks and tools for maintaining relationships. Feel the beginning of anger, use it for excitement. For what does evil exist at all? Any energy needs to be put to good use. Small malice: helps to enliven the situation, removes laziness, excites; and large: stuns, destroys the body, and reduces activity.

It is necessary to develop talent, the ability to stop negativity and switch to the love. Understand for yourself what you want – to live or be lazy? Do it yourself, and go further forward, live in independence, it is always with you.

There is another story when breaking up a relationship for an incapable partner is a thrill – freedom. Now, you can live and breathe, now you don't have to be afraid to talk, no one reads notations for hours; no one reproaches and walks around with that always gloomy and dissatisfied face, constantly grumbling under his breath or out loud his unflattering comments.

This is what can be brought to by constant dissatisfaction, showdown, lies, whining, remarks on trifles – yes, there is no end to this list that can bring to this last limit of relations, even the one who and whom loved very much and wanted to be together. Here is written the word loved in the past tense, because now there is no love, in its place to come indifference and fatigue. Many people think that when someone don't love you any more, just need to get up and leave, don't try to glue what has been shattered to smithereens, since such relationships are self-destruction, utopia.

Can are you help psychologists, psychics, friends and relatives, alcohol or going to the side for professional sex for the novelty of feelings? Perhaps, can, but why? What can be offered to a couple that no longer reaches out to each other and suffers?

Unfortunately, not everyone has the opportunity to

radically change their lives: a joint budget, house, children who need a full-fledged family. Taking into account the fact (in whole or in part) that each family member has his own individual needs, as well as common collective ones, then to raise a radical way the issue about termination of relations will not be unprofitable.

So what to do?

Need to like each other again. As you dive deeper into the conscious towards the horizon of infinite wisdom (feeling), you will find plenty of reasons to pick up and fix the situation of a broken relationship. From this moment on, all complex cases should to divide into simple ones, that is, resort to early experience of relationships – poetry and sex. Imagine how much time has passed since then. The history doesn't end there. That what will inevitably happen we will meet humanly – well for kindness, and the bad we will reduce up to the funny size. Don't waste your time alone, it's only great in a relationship. Love does not disappear; it turns into being in love that partners try to hide until one of them apologises and admits his mistakes. No mistakes – no happiness. This is what disguises itself and substitutes the feeling of love to pay with the destruction of relationships. So means, the key of clue is happiness.

Living together, partners analyse (destroy) their love and relationships trying to find the cause of discomfort, and it (cause) hide very close. The main enemy of happiness is laziness, avoidance of activity. Although love in our understanding is not an activity because it cannot be done – only registered, then the feeling of happiness must be earned by activity (correcting mistakes.) Therefore, there are happy single and happy married people. So, happiness can exist separately from love, this feeling is independent. And do not blame your partner for the lack of love; you did not lose love, but happiness, because of laziness.

Being in love and love for us are identical feelings that are never to blame for anything. And if you think that these are different feelings, then for you it really is. It is strange, but we do not feel the difference between being in love and love, either at the very beginning of the development of relationships or after years of living together. For us, love is – being in love, which arose from the colossal energy of the object / objects of love, and there is no particular reason to look for someone else's fault, which was written about earlier in the pages of this book. We are not able to simply take and betray that exceptional moment, tear it apart, split it into two different feelings: release on the left side some of the experiences, meanings, that are dear to us, and on the right side to mix some new experiences acquired after a while, where they will be there are duplicate feelings from the opposite left side, supplemented by free radicals that trigger the reaction of total mutation. Who knows where these mutating feelings will take you or throw you in the future? The meaning of love is predetermined at the very beginning of the relationship and therefore it cannot be otherwise.

Mutations of love feelings, every couple in love seeks to protect and strengthen their love from the outside world. But is it possible to do this, and most importantly, why? Does love need any protection? For our love, definitely not, but incredulous and doubting people say – yes. Therefore, let's tell them that any protective function complicates and slows down the system or relationships. Intervention in consciousness will inevitably lead the individual to a new emotional matrix. Created and loaded into memory a hybrid stimulus of love, a mutant, will be a dominant glitch that interferes with the perception of the primary feeling of love. By solving in this way the problem of how to secure love, couples in love actually move away from love. They are in the process of building a firewall use many different tricks: from warnings about etiquette and decent behaviour before the upcoming business trip, to organisation their own romantic evenings, from which, as they think, their feelings are strengthened. After a while, this activity begins a little to tire, there comes a period when both partners want to diversify their lives by searching for new emotions, sensations, and the cunning ones never create dangerous mutations of feelings.

Playing theatrically in front of each other, turning into good (positive,) then bad (negative) characters, our advice for you would be this: do not modify the primary basic experiences. That and is the unique main portal of connection in a relationship, everything else is colour photographs to brag and laugh heartily.

Distrustful persons install protection on this particular portal.

But what do they want to control and protect? Of course, the weak qualities of a person's nature, both of his own and his partner. Distrustful persons ruled by feelings of anxiety and suspicion, preventing them to enjoying love.

Question! What is preferable to do: change yourself or ask your partner to make efforts in this direction?

We complicate the condition of the problem as follows: the unknown is not a part, but our whole life.

Creating a protection system, a creative person will understand that all being developed the algorithms of actions will lead to a single function – a bodyguard, from which it is impossible to find love. This is a classic of relationship.

If to partner is not trusted, will he keep the portal opening? We assume he will be upset for the care, and access to love will be closed. The shown behaviour is copied and the feelings are mutated into new relationships.

So, the portal has closed, a huge reinforced concrete door has blocked access to feelings of love, and the partner reinsurer will have to do incredible things for that to crack the door and provide arguments for himself behaviour, hoping to regain trust and mutual understanding. Constructively, but is he really driven only by these needs? Perhaps, there is love in him. After listening to his sincere story explaining the reasons for the current situation and the proposed behaviour, now, it remains to compare all this with the facts and decides to forgive and open the portal of love. Need to give a person a new chance that for to look if it makes him and you a happy.

Fantasy! Only attentive people will see that the reinforced concrete door was built by the hands of the partner reinsurer, therefore he exactly knows all the drawings and specifications of his own creation, that is, have access to the main primary feelings. So, why does his need outside help in order to open this door to the portal of love?

It is immediately evident that he worked diligently, as they say in good faith, so that no one could reproach him for any inaccuracy. He does not need criticism; he is a professional – Mr Perfectionist. And here's a bummer, the door slammed from a weak breeze, because it became difficult for another partner to breathe in a closed world and he had to open the window. Just think a multi-ton door slammed shut from a draft. Probably the master really took a long time to calibrate the mechanism. His lack of competence was as follows; external doors always open outward so that people inside can leave the room at any time. It is this fatal mistake that requires outside help, such an anxious and suspicious partner reinsurer is dangerous – he must admit this and correct himself.

You know, we wanted to write about the owners in such an unusual way of interpretation. They had, in advance, to understand the meanings of the relationship and prepare their psyche for a balanced perception of the weak qualities of human nature.

Of course, she is beautiful and knows how to attract the attention of fans. It cannot be in any other way. Negotiations, attention, her laughter, and turns the partner owner's into a neurotic. Jealousy – many people suffer from this. Yes, what are we talking about if even sitting at the dinner table with close friends you notice strange things with her. Stroking legs while looking at the opposite sex or inexplicable hugs and kisses on the lips of their girlfriends. This is a very striking sexual behaviour aimed at overcoming the stress from a boring marriage? Sensitive persons, with the help of fantasy and imagination, begin to transfer this reality into speculation in the workplace, imagining it with one of the capable and easily tempted employees or customers. In relations, appears a stable appeal to the literary word b*.

For worse or better, who knows, maybe all relationships have a standard set of telepathic communication with periodic attacks of verbal revelation. In the world, there are things that we cannot understand and cannot overcome, even if the love of a partner says otherwise. Sexual energy exists, and dominates our behaviour. It cannot be underestimated and constantly distorted, disfigured by cloying caressing words or silence. The shock from natural words is programmed by ethics and the power of the meaning embedded in the turn of speech. People are most afraid of being simple; they want to put a lot of meaning into everything that surrounds us. From underwear and a car, to the level of preferences in the use of outer space, cool things are necessary for emphasise the line of self-expression, the signature of sexual energy, moreover not obligatory for everyday its implementation. Some of us like to feel sex inside self without expending energy. It is change the boring temperament into a dynamic and secretive behaviour. When a person has a reserve of energy, he uses one single model of behaviour – to find a way how to consume this energy in an unusual way – especially, that to script are some cool moments and unexpected surprises.

Here, the individual has no right to make a mistake, if this condition is not achieved, then the pleasure from the spent energy will not be received.

Disappointment in the topic of sex should not be. Nobody wants hysterics. Let's think about what attributes are associated with first-class sex. We will call them directly as they are, without boring abstruse phrases like a demonstration of sexual behaviour and etc.

So let's start: Office business clothes – jacket, tie, blouse, stockings, and shoes. Underwear, skirt or trousers are a barrier and therefore cannot be classified in this category; Music; Gifts, including chocolate; Conversations on various topics; Stroking with hands; Embraces; Kisses; Inviting gestures; Dancing; Photo and video shooting; Striptease; Jacuzzi; Massage; Bed, sofa; Ceiling with the effect of the starry sky. Yes, this list ask the funding and we work every day for aspire to realise our own dreams. Imagine how cool in the evening to relax in the Jacuzzi, so many tempting options opening in front of you. For example,

– to dive shoulder-deep into water in together for five minutes, then someone of them can to rise higher...

Bliss! The purest water and no chemistry – this is nature. He settled down opposite her and waits for her caresses. She will do cool things with him – she is nature in the guise of energetic beauty, and he is a victim trying to dominate her, and get aroused from it. Of course, he needs help from her, otherwise, without this condition; sexual energy will be converted into related feelings from an unfinished action. Sex is the topic from which it is impossible to leave the winner or the vanquished. «I was on top of» – it is a very common expression from the eighties of the last century emphasising the boasting of the mastery of sexual abilities, and it is wrong. The intimate theme is always low and new. Humans don't have the adaptability, skills, or insurance to it. For example, married couples often have situations when sex brings less and less those earlier sensual experiences.

Risk is an integral part of any relationship and connection, and it is not necessary to argue that without trust doesn't surface the love. People adore and love everything and everyone around. Curiosity and the need for emotion make them be led to stupidity. I trusted you so much, and you unfaithfulness (betrayed) me! Bad, terrible, go away.

Did he leave or stay, the question is what did you like about this event?

Nothing!

Pain, longing, the desire to teach a lesson or brag about your achievements, but while you are punishing yourself with your anxious behaviour, you indirectly admit that you missed the chance to live a happy life together. And what was the mistake; he was weak-willed and never appreciated your feelings? This happens when one partner trusts another, hoping that he will change for the better, stop deceiving and scandalizing.

It's funny, moving away from this topic half a step aside, you can feel the statement that without trust love does not arise – yet it does! Try to search near you're at home, on the street, and almost anywhere you can imagine, and we will wait a bit.

Did you find an answer? These are pet owners who love their pets even when those scratch and bite. Pet owners love the expression, surprise and unpredictability of friendly moments. To notice, that in this example, not some known force will not make break their love, because the relationship is held by the main primary feelings (small, beautiful, fluffy, meows, scratches, barks, bites).

Do you know how many people in the world experience fear when they try to fall asleep in bed imagining that somewhere nearby is sneaking their unpredictable four-legged friend? There is no trust, but there is love. Strange pleasure or deceit!

Suspicions to the maximum, the red light flashes, the siren generates a sound wave of one hundred decibels and the partner with a beaming smile on his face asks: What?

Nonsense is the best topic. Where is stupidity, there I am, this is my Rock&Roll. Is it possible to deprive a person of stupidity? All human activity is aimed at the development of stupidity. People to make an effort from ability to ability, and then the Universe will split what remains of us into negligible amounts.

Are you one of those who experience angular acceleration towards the black hole at the centre of our galaxy? Then, welcome to our club of the extraterrestrial romantics. Every evening we build a spaceship for to leave the dangerous world and, like a good-natured Hippies in their time, we also wish Earthlings to find peace and love.

Excuse me, but on which TV channel will be broadcast the entertainment programme – «a Kiss at parting» To smack one's lips and bye, thank you for your attention.

Really, that quickly relationships go to the end?

They are definitely champions by stupidity. Even our alien technology does not allow transmission of signals as fast as among some special couples. They are shaking at close range distance from each other, invisible energy pervading space and hitting the target.

It works like this – one partner with a directed look «drills» another partner. The brain and the central nervous system cannot withstand the load; appear harmonically positive and harmonically negative waves which bring the individual into a rave seizure. Maybe, that is why in some musical directions there are few texts about happy love?

And we have Rock&Roll. It is fun and cool. A natural body without synthetics, bright smiles and no thoughts to close has just begun day. Love leaves and comes, and we meet and see it off every day, and it doesn't matter on what accessible principle it is operation at you (virtually-imaginary personal fantasy of the individual; physical; psychological-mutual; or any other). The main thing is to understand that only this our body can work.

Have notice that synthetics destroy relationships. This is a deception, a desire to quickly jump over friendship into a love relationship. Look at a photo taken according to the rules of seduction – in makeup, sexy clothes and a profitable perspective. The theme of love and being in love immediately slide into consumption, that is intimacy. Invested in this way, the initial meaning of the relationship will be too bright for a comfortable family life. Sex warms hot and creates discomfort. It is very difficult to live with a person from whom you feel an incredible level of eroticism and sexuality. It can cause anything, and the beauty of the body, and a special exciting voice, demeanor, associations, thoughts and inexplicable (invisible) energy.

Question: What do you think, what primary arise in a person is being in love or love?

We affirm this is love. Without love, it is impossible to have a cool feeling of being in love. Therefore, there is a mistake in many psychological studies that claim that being in love arises only with sexual feelings, which after a while can develop into love.

At the beginning arises love. A person perceives the object of being in love at the level of not just sympathy, but at the level of love, and only after that an «ultra-short impulse» triggers the physiological mechanism of the state of being in love.

Without this condition (instant verification of the matrix of our own wishes with the object of love) our brain simply will not allow to take an indefinite risk and start the mechanism of being in love.

What is the reason to have a falling (being) in love to object, if you don't love that object?

The answer is simple: – Only the need for sex.

One of the famous thinkers of the past *Thomas Aquinas* (1225), an Italian philosopher, claimed that «Love is term of knowledge» and «Unknown cannot be loved»

Continuing his train of thought, one can point out that

although people love the secrets and mysteries of the universe, but this does not allow one to approach the love of what is unknown. Let's say, we love the universe, but there are many unknowns in it. The closest experience, in this case, will be love for the process of searching for secrets and riddles. Or like this: we love a person, but his body is not a topic for the faint of heart.

Is it correct to look for love from the general to the specific? After all, people are a complex indivisible system and therefore it is ridiculous, or rather doubtful, to talk about love for specific parts of the body or skills, abilities, thinking. True or false this it!

I love your hands, they are tender and beautiful; I love your mind; I love you for being a great driver; I don't love you because I don't know everything about you – solid secrets, riddles, the unknown; I love you wholly.

It is provocative and useful to think about relationships in this perspective.

Now, let's return to the development of our idea about what comes first: being in love or love? In our statement there is the following logic – the first a love, because you have already instantly studied the object of love and left a little intrigue for future knowledge, for example: in morality, in sex, in creating a family, and for this you need to turn on in the body special emotional knowledge – being in love. With the help of it, the individual easily breaks through any defence and receives interest information from the object of love (about the profession, habits, interests, hobbies, and so on).

Such information from the point of view of the importance of the being created relationship is secondary, insignificant. Understand, there was an amazing coincidence, just think, one chance in a million! You really don't trust your flair?

Scanning an object in milliseconds, is it even possible?

Yes. Vision allows you to see through a person, hearing determines the health and development of an interest object, the energy field is recorded by responsible receptors...and the answer is ready.

Like, but yet this is not love. So, this is not that case. You are what expecting? Some kind of event, that is, special behaviour from a partner, then what are you going to love? Actions – acts, a gifts or a partner?

We drove; it's a hard to be a dubious person? Leave the partner alone, he deserves more with someone else, one-sided love is definitely not enough for two.

Loneliness! Usually people think like this: «I am sad and I will never be able to meet my love» or «cool, I'm finally free» It's funny, but we see a different point of view in this. There are four personal behaviours of loneliness: the first – is perfectionist persons who strive for accuracy, punctuality, including faithful widowed monogamous people who keep love in their hearts; the second – is passive persons who wish to be lazy; the third – is limited persons who do not have sufficient strength or condition to realise their dream of finding a full-fledged relationship; fourth – these are conflicting persons who consciously isolate themselves (or with help others) due to the inability to control their strength, anger. Do you know what they all have in common (except for widowed monogamous and limited persons) the search for even more stupidity than those people who are looking for love?

In loneliness, our surrounding world turns into a emptiness. And this is a direct road to self-sufficiency, selfishness. There is a mistake of thinking, in the emptiness it is not possible to find even stupidity without talking about something else. Self-sufficient people create this emptiness; these are closed systems consuming the resources of the planet. They live according to the logic of the procedure, get what they need and nothing return back. As you gain independence, be prepared for colossal psychological changes. You have to change your humanity and go through the rite of depersonalization, erasing all traces, running away from yourself. However, capable people become self-sufficient and boast of life achievements. They also want to succeed in relationships. This is cannot be. They consume relations and do not unite people for friendship, love and communication.

By logically, for self-sufficient person does not need anyone. There is a leading phrase: I alone have achieved everything that I have, and it's cool! This is the most natural selfishness and lies. It is a pity those heads on which such a person passed.

At the same time and modest single individuals with minimal demands also choose the wrong path of development. Perhaps they carefully keep from others what they earn with great difficulty that was achieved on their own without having the desired support from other people...

So, people need their own world built inside our common big world. What for? To acquire even greater uniqueness, and for this, there is no need to isolate yourself by loneliness, except for especially regular cases – going to the restroom.

Turbo love or modern romance! Airport, a departure hall, a lot of fussy people, and among them there are several energy persons who are in the erotic dimension. Our world for them is erotica and fetishism. They pick up the notes of attraction at great distance and enter into a confidential contact after a few simple words. This is magic, telepathic communication, endlessly vivid sexual behaviour, exactly the kind that was programmed by your body for yourself. You literally feel the energy from the interlocutor or from an object that is out of line of sight. That is where you really want to argue that you can fall in love, or rather the one which you don't know. Maybe, this is known to science the chemistry of love – a pheromone path left by someone, but this is not that. This is an insight, a rock of fate; perhaps, this is an intermediary who has the task of conveying something to you from another world. Adapt starts the game, appears intrigue, the unknown forces him to explore a new world. Telepathic contact captures the target and both of them are already standing opposite each other and know that the current dialogue is just etiquette, a cover for sexual desires from the outside world...

Conclusion

Eureka, so will say the inhabitants of the Earth. We wrote a book about love in a new interpretation for you, without jam, without sugary and overly caring approach. All this work is a thinking of two very close people. One of us chose a precise professional approach, knowledge from the field of psychology and corresponding sciences, not wanting to invest and publish his personal experience, and the other strove for the opposite.

By exposing this fact to publicity, we would like to reveal to you another secret. Actually, originally was written a completely different book than this. In the first version, as not strange it now sounds, there was no itself love.

Statistics, the controversy of famous scientists squeezed by the framework of etiquette and much more did not allow creating a book focused on easier reading.

Therefore, we had to temporarily break creative cooperation. This moment of life really put the relationship under the verification of primary feelings. Insurmountable disagreements and increased emotional background were accompanied for nearly one year. If try to describe the received experiences, then this can be compared with the desire to analyse our lived years, reproaches and achievements to which we came together.

And the result was really sad, on the desk lay a boring lifeless scientific book, which apparently is reflection of two completely different strangers, and with all this needed to do something.

And we decided to switch roles based on only one single rule that states that only in love can be created an interesting project. This creativity has captured us. Now, emotional of knowledge and thinking dominated over dry logic, and the new book slowly began to grow page by page. Intuition prompted the authors answer to unknown at that time questions. This entire book was written impromptu. We did not limit love to anything. Imagine a white sheet of paper in front of you, fill it out.

So, what is love? This, in including, an intimate attraction and not unlimited tenderness; Yes, we not slip of the pen, tenderness cannot be limitless, at the ends of tenderness there is always presence a pain.

Homo sapiens are also a myth, the wrong wording. The needs for emotions and feelings are the initiators of behaviour and thinking. Therefore, it would be more correct to say: «Homo is not predictable»

Some of us, in order to control own behaviour do not strive to immerse experiences deep in self. And it's very strange. There is clearly making a mistake here. There is no depth of feeling in love. It is unchanging. Only people thought up exactly for themselves to evaluate feelings in their own way, appropriating certain attributes and meanings with the effect of the strength of experiences, responsibility, care and much more.

As seems to us, wildly to try doing some stupid levels of love in head and rating it like a product in a store.

Love is either there or not, and it is very good that it plays with us every day. Know how to forgive your logical thinking that interfere to life, and you will find harmony and happiness.

Our respect.